INCIDENTAL DAUGHTER

Val Stasik

Armery & Hallquist Publishing

Santa Fe, New Mexico

Armery & Hallquist Publishing, Santa Fe, New Mexico
Copyright © 2013 Valerie W. Stasik
All rights reserved. Published 2013
ISBN–10: 0988584700
ISBN–13: 978-0-9885847-0-9

To Louis Shapiro,
1964–66 University of Pittsburgh
English professor who believed in
the freshman from Podunk.

If wishes were horses, beggars would ride.

—James Kelly, *Scottish Proverbs,
Collected and Arranged*

~❦~**ONE**~❦~

A FAMILIAR BELLOWING in the outer office captured Liz Michael's attention. She slipped the contract for the purchase of William Penn Press back into its folder and navigated through the precisely-stacked piles of manuscripts to lift a slat of the blinds covering the door and floor-to-ceiling windows that faced the outer office. Addy Payne strained toward Mandy, pounded her desk, and demanded to see Liz. Paper clips, pens, and papers flew off her desk like hard rain.

Liz glanced at her watch. Only 2:17, but the flush of booze had already spread from her ex-husband's face to his scalp in sharp contrast to his sleek, white-blond hair. This bloated caricature was not the man she had once loved. She shook her head. No, she could not possibly have fallen in love with that.

As he headed for her office, trailed by Mandy, Liz considered escaping through the other door in her office, but she knew he'd keep coming back—best to deal with him now. She whirled back to her desk, sat, and pretended to peruse the documents in the William Penn Press folder. Addy whipped the door open, but held it, and peered at Mandy as though she were the intruder. Mandy's hazel eyes pleaded with Liz, and she shrugged her plump shoulders.

"It's okay, Mandy. Call Miriam and tell her I'll have the contract ready for her before four."

Mandy scurried out of the room like a rabbit frantic for cover. Addy smiled, shook his head, and closed the door. He removed a stack of manuscripts from a tan guest chair, sat, and adjusted his perfectly pressed pants. "You look well," he said.

Liz stood, marched to the blinds, and opened them. Mandy glanced up from her phone call to Miriam and nodded her readiness to call security at Liz's signal. Liz returned to her desk, sat, folded her hands, and calmly stared at him a moment. "What brings you here today, Addy?"

He glanced back at the open blinds, raised his brows, and looked back at her with a slow, feline smile. "What? No 'How are you? It's good to see you, Addy.'"

Liz stared back at him, unsmiling.

He shook his head. "Poor sales technique, Lizzie."

"I'm not selling anything. What do you want? I'm busy."

Addy glanced at the stacks of manuscripts and nodded. "I can see that. You used to be a lot neater."

She continued to stare.

He relaxed back into the chair, placed a leg over his knee, and rested his hands on the arms of the chair in one graceful movement. He considered her a moment. "I need money."

"You're wasting my time. Get a job."

His gray eyes darkened. "Pittsburgh isn't exactly the center of the advertising world."

"Not my problem. I told you the last time, no more loans—as if I'll ever see the money I've already given you." She cocked her head to one side. "Tell me, Addy, whatever happened to all of your contacts? Why don't you go to your family?"

He looked away from her and studied the awards on one wall and then the print of Cassatt's "The Boating Party" on the opposite wall. The muffled ring of Mandy's phone in the outer office underscored the silence.

"They don't know, do they? They think you're still the Great Ad Man, pulling off one outrageous magic trick after another."

He returned his gaze to her. "I want to start my own agency."

She gave him a tight-lipped smile and shook her head. "You don't know you've dropped off the edge, do you? You had quite a run taking risks with your accounts. . . . Oh, you had us all fooled. Me. Your clients. We thought your three-martini lunches fueled your success, till your lack of follow-through took everything south. . . . Lay off the booze, Addy. Then go to New York, LA, Chicago. Find a job with an agency where they don't know you."

His whole body deflated. "It's been too long since the last job. Even if I were hired, I'd have to start at the bottom."

Liz leaned back in her chair. "Screwed everybody who could give you a good reference, huh? Why don't you try something else? Maybe banking? Or drive a cab? Who knows? You could end up head of the company."

He looked worse than he had the last time if that was possible. Now that he was sitting across from her, she could see tiny veins were beginning to sprout on his nose. "By the way, as I've said many times, AA has quite a history for turning people's lives around. Why don't you give them a try? What could it hurt?"

He sprang from his chair and, hands fisted, leaned on her desk. She scowled at the stink of whiskey on his breath. "Look, I'm not some jerk barfly from a dirty Pennsylvania steel town." His eyes bulged. "You know I come from one of the oldest families in Ohio. I have an MBA from Harvard. I've made three different agencies big money. And I know I can create the best ad agency this town that thinks it's a city has ever seen."

Liz rose from her desk. "Then I suggest you create a business plan—they did teach you how to write a business plan at Harvard, didn't they—and take it to the bank for a loan."

She jerked the hem of her linen jacket. "Now, I have work to do." She strode to the door, but before she could open it, he grabbed her arm.

"You've never forgiven me, have you?

She froze, her face a rigid mask. "Let go of me."

Addy freed her and she opened the door. He left without another word.

⚘TWO⚘

"NO, MANDY. LIZ is quite capable of taking care of herself. Call security only if she signals you to do so. Of course, if Payne appears threatening, get somebody up here right away. Please call me when he's left."

Miriam Kernan returned to the intern application. She nodded, and a smile crept onto her face.

Ah, yes, the past finds us when we least expect it.

Miriam's own past had intruded into her life recently, an opportunity that would allow her to bring a little justice into the world. Perhaps this incursion from Liz's past would be her opportunity for justice, for healing. Liz claimed to be content, but Miriam sometimes spied her staring at the Cassatt print of the man, woman, and child in a small sailboat that hung on a wall in her office. Would she disappear into that print of a close knit family if she could? And which would she be—the woman or the child?

Miriam pressed the intercom button. "Martha, send in the intern candidate."

When her door opened, she removed her reading glasses and glanced at the slender young man who nodded and greeted her before installing himself in the chair in front of her desk. His navy blazer opened over a pale blue shirt and a slightly askew tan striped tie. He settled his long legs and sat straight but unperturbed. Paddy Arnesson was not the least bit intimidated by the luxurious antique furnishings of her office—or her.

Yes, just like Liz, he has a strong sense of self.

He brushed back the lock of dark hair that kept falling over his forehead.

Ah, yes, he is one of that breed of Irishmen referred to as Black Irish, not a redhead like my Gerald. Some say they descend from some Spaniards from the Spanish Armada. Spaniards? Why not Jewish merchants? Yes, except for the dark hair, he would definitely pass for Liz's brother. The space between his teeth confirms it.

"I'm curious, I see the name on your application is 'Ivar Arnesson,' but you go by 'Paddy.' Where does that come from?"

His smile crinkled his eyes. "I was born on March seventeenth."

"Oh, yes. St. Patrick's Day."

"Since my parents decided I'd be their last child, and I'm the only boy, they named me after my father. They didn't want to call me 'Junior,' though, so everyone calls me Paddy. My dad was Swedish, but Mom's Irish."

Miriam nodded and leaned back in her chair. "So, you want to be a writer?"

"Since I was twelve."

"That's pretty young to know what you want to do with your life."

"My seventh grade English teacher turned me on to writing."

"And how did she do that?"

"We did a lot of writing, and she worked with each of us individually. When she read my first story, she asked me where I got the idea. I found out much later that it was very similar to Sartre's play, *No Exit*. I think she thought I must have seen it and used the idea, but she never accused me of plagiarism."

"And did you borrow from that play?"

His eyes widened. "No! Back then, I'd never even seen a professional play. Dad didn't know about that play either. He thought it was a great story and told me he was proud of me. I think Mom knew it was similar, but she never said anything—probably didn't want to give me a big head."

Miriam looked pleased and nodded.

"My teacher worked with me a lot, and I learned so much from her." He blushed, lowered his eyes, and then looked up. "She told me I had talent, that I should always write, even if it was only a hobby. She said I'd always feel a little hollow inside if I didn't."

"Hm, yes. Her recommendation left me thinking you could be the next Steinbeck." Miriam was pleased to see that Paddy had the grace to blush again. "I happen to know her very well, and she usually knows what she's talking about."

He cocked his head.

"We've published a number of her books."

"But I've never—"

"She uses a pseudonym."

His face split into a huge grin. "Right on, Ms. Brunet!"

Miriam laughed and glanced down at his application. "You indicate that you've been published—some school lit magazines, a few contests, and—most impressive—a piece in *Penwell*. You must be one of the youngest contributors they've published."

His pale skin flushed again. "I was seventeen when they accepted it."

"Hm. Not so long ago. Tell me about your work. Who does your editing? Things like that."

He told her he did most of his editing as he wrote, but admitted to a few all-nighters when he couldn't get an extension on an assignment that needed more revising.

"Have you submitted many pieces for publication?"

He rolled his eyes. "Oh yeah. Tons!"

"So, you're no stranger to rejection slips?"

"Wall's papered with them, but I keep writing."

"That's good. Ever sent a manuscript to us?"

"No. I'm working on my first novel, though."

"Well, whether or not you are awarded an apprenticeship, I'd like you to send me some of your published pieces. Be sure to include the *Penwell* piece. And send me the first three chapters of your book with a synopsis of the rest. I don't want Ms. Brunet shaking her finger at me because we missed the boat not publishing you if you do turn out to be your generation's Steinbeck. . . . On second thought, forget the synopsis. Send me the whole manuscript."

"I'm only on the third draft."

Miriam pulled open a file drawer and wrestled a sheet from one of the files. "I'm sure we will be able to tell if it's publishable from a third draft. I will be sharing it with our senior editor, Liz Michaels." She glanced at his face but saw no hint of recognition. She then penned checks by a few of the entries on the sheet. "In the meantime, here is a list of agents. I've marked ones that have worked well with us and do a good job of looking after their clients. You may say I recommended them. Just to keep everyone honest, you should always have representation. They are accustomed to being interviewed, so choose someone you feel understands you and your writing." She handed him the sheet.

"Mrs. Kernan, I don't know what to say. Thanks!"

"Must be your Swedish side. The Irish are never at a loss for words."

ᏋᏗᎿTHREEᏗᎨ

LIZ NEARLY COLLIDED with a young man leaving Miriam's office. He excused himself and smiled at her. That smile stopped her a moment. There was something familiar about him, but she couldn't think why that might be, and he was gone before she could ask him if they had met before. She shrugged, entered Miriam's office, and handed her the file for William Penn Press.

"I've added a clause to the contract requiring Abe Perkins to remain on site two days a week the first year and as an off-site consultant for the following two years, with appropriate compensation, of course. Gerald and I can work that out with him before we finalize the sale," Liz said.

Miriam finished scanning all the other changes Liz had made and looked up at her. "You know, he might balk at being on site for a year. They're moving to Florida as soon as they can after the sale."

"We need to have a smooth transition if we want to preserve William Penn Press's traditions. I know that's a big concern of his, so I'll emphasize how important his input will be to accomplish that." Liz smiled. "Anyway, that house they're building in Naples may take another year or longer before it's ready. You know how Abe's wife is about changing things at the last minute."

"True, and I know how persuasive you and Gerald are. By the way, what did your suave ex-husband want? Mandy said he left rather abruptly."

"The same as always—money. He thinks he can start his own ad agency."

"That Shaker Heights *schlemiel* has family with money. Why doesn't he go to them?"

"Not even his mother knows he's been out of work so long. He would die before letting them see how he's screwed up."

"Arrogance, too many risks, and too much alcohol—a recipe for failure."

"I told him it wasn't my problem, and he should get help for his drinking, go elsewhere, and start over. But Addy is not one to admit he has a problem or start from scratch."

"And so he expects you to be there for him, even though he wasn't there for you when you needed him the most."

"Isn't that the way of a narcissist?"

"Well, we'll alert security not to let him up here again."

"Aw, Miriam, Addy goes wherever he wants. I can't worry about him. Don't bother security."

"If you say so." She lifted a folder and handed it to Liz. "I think you should see this."

"What is it?"

"The application of one of the intern candidates."

When Liz saw the name on the folder, she sat down and said nothing for a few moments, only stared at the folder. Then she raised stony eyes to Miriam. "Was that who just left your office?"

Miriam nodded. "Read his application."

Liz did so, finished after a long perusal, and regarded Miriam with a frown. "Of all the publishers, why us?"

"Why not us? We set the standard in Pittsburgh and have a reputation for grooming talent. The others make gofers out of their interns."

Liz bit her lip. "Do you think my father told his family about me after all?"

"If he had, wouldn't they have insisted on meeting you?"

She glowered. "From the way he reacted, I don't think his wife would have been happy about me."

"I mentioned your name in passing, and he didn't react."

"They might not know I no longer go by 'Migielski.' Of course, it's a matter of public record—if they cared to check." Liz dropped the file on Miriam's desk. "Well, if this boy is what we're looking for, don't hold the past against him. On the other hand, don't give him an internship because he's my brother. . . . I probably won't run into him anyway."

※

Miriam stared at the door for a very long time after Liz left. It was incredible to see this sophisticated professional woman revert to the wounded nineteen-year-old she had once been. Miriam drummed her fingers on the desk. It was long past time for Liz to rid herself of old hurts, time to vanquish old ghosts and live in the light—just as Miriam had.

ᏋᎿᎿ**FOUR**ᏋᏋ

ADDY HEADED FOR Busch's Tavern. Aside from running multiple tabs without any of them getting too high, one of the perks of frequenting so many of these watering holes was the pool of resourceful drinkers he might not otherwise have met. Virgil was one of these talents who promised him something very special. It was part of Addy's contingency plan, labeled as such in his flow chart in case Liz refused him the loan. Besides, when Busch wasn't around, Emily sometimes refilled his flask without adding it to Addy's tab. He always slipped her a few ones with the smile and melting eyes of a film idol.

The tavern was located in what had once been a 1940s drugstore and soda fountain on the Southside; really a long, narrow room with a bar on one side, booths on the other, and a few scattered tables between. An office, storage room, and restrooms at the back completed the area. The place suited the neighborhood locals just fine. Addy was one of maybe three outsiders who sometimes frequented the bar. Aside from the freebies, he liked the place because he could park his black Jag right out front where he could keep an eye on it. That ride was crucial to his image. He was still a player—just having a little run of bad luck.

His eyes soon adjusted to the dimly-lit bar, but he'd never get used to the odors of stale beer, Camel cigarettes, roasted peanuts, and disinfectant that did little to disguise the sulfurous aroma from the restrooms. A small TV high up over a corner of the bar, sound turned low, played some sports program no one was watching.

The bulk of Del Busch loomed over Emily, the woman working the bar. Stringy, bleached hair restrained by a black headband fluttered as she nodded. She rarely raised her eyes to the man who seemed to be giving her unwelcome orders. When he was finished, she looked up with watery blue eyes and spotted Addy. She smiled a welcome that revealed over-sized dentures. Unfortunately, her smile only served to make her face pucker and wrinkle as though she'd been sucking a lemon.

"Addy!"

He managed not to wince at her squeaky-door voice. Busch turned and glared at him. He then masked his distaste with a stiff smile and a wave. "Hey, how's the *Hahvahd* man?" He glanced out at Addy's car parked right in front of his tavern. "See you're still driving that chick magnet."

"Not so much for the babes, Del. It's a tool of the trade in my line of work."

Still staring at the Jaguar, Busch nodded like a bobble-headed doll. "Yeah, your work. How's that going, anyway?"

"Oh good! Good. Big things happening in the next couple of days."

"Ya don't say? Glad to hear it." He turned to leave and looked hard at Emily. "Then maybe you can take care of your tab." Without waiting for an answer, he strolled back to his office.

"Hey, sweetheart, how about pouring me a double shot of Maker's Mark, no ice?"

Her smile disappeared. "Busch says you gotta pay some on your tab. You know if it was up to me, I'd let it ride."

Addy rolled his eyes and sighed. "What's the damage?"

Emily paged through a small notebook. "Gee, it is pretty high. $78.67."

Considering how little Busch charged, Addy had done quite a lot of drinking here, not including the free flask refills. He pulled out his wallet and fanned the bundle of mostly ones, fives, and tens—$558, all he had for the next two weeks, and he still had to pay Virgil.

He looked at her the way he always did, a twinkle in his pale eyes. "How about thirty-five?"

Emily looked at him like a kid who'd lost her puppy and shook her head. "Busch said at least fifty."

Addy peeled off four tens and ten ones. "Okay, here you go."

Her sour smile reappeared and she took the money, entering the payment in the notebook. "We're out of Maker's Mark. How about Wild Turkey?"

It was all he could do to keep from blanching, but, hey, whiskey was whiskey, and it was a lot cheaper than Maker's Mark, so it wouldn't inflate his tab so much. Besides, he wanted to get his deal done with Virgil. Addy had seen him in the back booth when he strolled in. "Sure."

Glass in hand, he headed for Virgil. The skinny, middle-aged, balding man still wore his gray janitor uniform—pretty clean, considering he kept the local police precinct in order. Virgil compensated for his minimum-wage salary by occasionally acquiring what he called "happy finds."

Addy slid into the seat across from Virgil "Do you have it?"

Virgil regarded him with pale brown eyes. "You have the money?"

Addy pulled out his wallet and counted out the bills. "Yeah, here's the fifty."

Virgil shook his head. "No. A hundred. I took a lot of chances to get this lock pick set."

Addy stared at the little man and calculated his next move. "Look, a deal's a deal. We agreed on fifty."

"So go buy one from a locksmith. I figure the only reason you're getting it from me is you don't want no record. Take it or leave it."

Addy pocketed his wallet, threw back his whiskey in one gulp, slid out of the booth, hitched up his pants, and turned to leave.

"Hey, let's talk," Virgil called after him.

"What's to talk about?" Addy answered without turning around.

"Don't you need this?" He glanced around to see if any of the other drinkers heard him.

Addy shrugged his shoulders and made as if to continue his exit; but Busch came from the back with a bottle of Maker's Mark and placed it on the shelf with the rest of the liquors. He then disappeared into his back office again without a word. Emily grabbed the Maker's Mark, glanced at Addy with a grin, and held out her hand. He crossed to the bar and handed her his flask.

Virgil scuttled to his side. "Okay, okay." He glanced around again and then held out the set to Addy.

Addy also scanned the bar before taking the set, but the few drinkers scattered around the smoky room seemed focused on some scene in their glasses. He passed over the fifty. Virgil kept his back to the room and counted it. Satisfied, he scurried back to his booth.

Emily finished topping off Addy's flask with the Maker's Mark and handed it to him. "How lucky was that?" she squeaked. "Didn't see any Maker's Mark when I looked in the storage room earlier. Seal's broken. Busch must've been having a snort back in his office."

"Emily, you are a real sweetheart."

She grinned, and Addy palmed her a couple of dollars. He headed to the door but glanced back at her and winked. Emily raised her reddened hand and gave him a tiny wave.

When Addy pulled away in his Jaguar, Virgil got up to chat with Emily but sat back down again when Busch strode out from his office. The hefty man, strands of dark hair combed over the bald top of his head, reached into Emily's pocket and seized Addy's tip. Emily stiffened at the coldness in his eyes.

"I'll take this—and I'll take one week's pay for all the free liquor you been giving that leech. Just be happy I don't fire you."

Everyone in the bar had to be furniture not to hear what he said. Emily, pink and wide-eyed, said nothing. Virgil glared at Busch.

"Now go clean the bathrooms and, this time, do it right."

After she scurried off to do his bidding, Busch grabbed the bottle of Maker's Mark and, frowning, held it over the sink, ready to pour. He looked around to see if anyone was looking, met Virgil's stare, and instantly capped the bottle. He then snatched a glass from the bar and sauntered back to his office.

Sometime later, he returned with the bottle and replaced it on the shelf. Virgil stared at him, barely blinking. Busch raised his hand and cocked it at him like it was a gun. Then the big man huffed a laugh. Virgil jerked his eyes back to his drink and looked into it for the future that was just out of reach.

৫৯৫FIVE৫৯৫

ADDY LEANED AGAINST one of the columns gracing the broad portico of Liz's building. This was not the home they had shared. However, it was a residence that would have suited Addy if he'd had the money to live there. Manicured cypress trees filled the areas at the sides of the portico and on the landscaped island bordering the wide, covered drive.

The Lafayette, a five-story, pale granite building astride Mt. Washington was the newest and largest high-end co-op in the entire city. The residents on the top floor facing the city side enjoyed a spectacular view, for which they paid a significant premium. The building allowed those top units a deep balcony terrace large enough to host a party of twenty. The terraces remained private since huge gaps separated them, and high walls at the sides blocked the view of neighboring units. So large was the building that it could easily have accommodated three times as many less lavish units.

From his hiding place, he looked across the drive through the building's glass doors. The gray-haired concierge who had ejected him from the building the previous week gestured at the doors and elevators for the benefit of another uniformed employee. The other man nodded, stepped out the door, and jogged to his car. The concierge occupied himself with arranging papers at the desk and answering the phone. With only the old guy on duty, Addy might sneak by him. However, the other guy returned carrying a little lunch cooler and a magazine tucked under his arm.

No way to get by the royal guard now.

The two talked further, and then the concierge headed for the doors. Addy retreated out of sight to one of the cypress trees and peered around it. The concierge pulled a set of keys from his pocket and headed for the parking lot.

Ah, going out for lunch, today? Good.

Once the old man drove out of the lot, Addy resumed his place behind the column. The young guy at the desk settled in and opened his lunch. Then, after glancing around the lobby, he pulled out his magazine. It looked like it might be *Playboy* or *Penthouse*.

Addy took a few swigs from his flask, and his pulse raced.

Wow! Haven't felt this great in a long time.

When he was sure the man was completely engaged with this month's Barbie doll replicas, he slipped through the glass doors and raced to the fire door on crepe-soled loafers. Liz's unit was on the top floor, but taking an elevator would have drawn too much attention. He inhaled the ever-present scent of hyacinth in the lobby and reached for the handle.

"Oh, no, you gotta be kidding!"

Addy froze and glanced at the desk only to realize it was not he but the enticing centerfold that had provoked the young man's exclamation. He hustled through the fire door, and, despite the fact that he was really out of shape, he made it to her floor without having to stop and catch his breath. Addy wondered at the adrenaline rush he felt but was grateful for it.

He peered through the little mesh window in the door to make sure no one was in the hall. He didn't want anyone to see him who might later remember passing a good-looking blond man. He tested the handle to make sure the fire door was unlocked.

His heart was now pounding so heavily that he could feel it in his ears. He fingered the lock pick set in his pocket, pressed through the fire door, and made a beeline down the burgundy plush-carpeted hall to the double doors of Liz's apartment.

After a few tries, Addy found the pick that freed the lock just as he heard the door of a unit down the hall opening. He managed to slip into Liz's apartment without being seen and engaged the lock. He turned, and the panoramic view of the Golden Triangle beyond the enormous terrace mesmerized him. The floor to ceiling windows of the living room had to be at least fifteen feet high.

Although he'd never seen her place and had more urgent things on his mind than exploring it now, he remembered the floor plan from the two-page newspaper spread that had come out for months when the units were being sold. In addition to this spacious living room, there was an en suite master, a guest room, a guest bath, a full kitchen, and a generous dining room. A wide gallery walkway from the foyer to the dining room flanked a wall that hid the kitchen and butler's pantry. Both the foyer and the dining room overlooked the living room, which could be reached by a flight of three steps from either end of the gallery. A waist-high ironwork railing along the gallery guarded against any chance of falling into the living room. He sighed. One of these aeries could have been his if his luck hadn't turned.

She still had Marisol's painting of a man, woman, and child in a boat hanging above the black granite fireplace. Marisol had titled it "The Boating Party" because Mary Cassatt's painting of the same name inspired it. The dark-haired, saucy Marisol was maid of honor at their wedding. Another time, another place, he would have done a little exploring with the little Spic from Santa Fe; however, he didn't much care for her paintings.

When Liz became pregnant, Marisol sent her the painting. Liz had burst into tears when she uncrated it. In the painting, the man and woman in the boat hovered over the child. The boat resembled a shallow nest floating on a mirror-like stream reflecting the threesome. Kind faces of old women were barely suggested in the trees along the bank and in the clouds. You really had to look to see them, but they were there.

Weird—fluffy, weird crapola. It was the only thing aside from her clothing Liz took when she left him.

The pregnancy. Babies didn't fit into his plans; she wasn't supposed to get pregnant when he was busy making it. In fact, he would have been just fine if she never got pregnant. Anyway, how could he be faulted for being out of town when she had the miscarriage? Then there were the months of depression when she wouldn't let him come near her. Hell, she'd only been pregnant for three months. It wasn't even really a baby. Besides, he didn't have the time and energy for boo-hooing. The pressure finally got to be too much, and he found the release he needed in greater quantities of alcohol, not to mention a one-night tryst whenever he could get away with it.

The memories of her unfairness used to make him angry, but today they didn't faze him at all. He was focused, really focused, on getting this job done. Today, she would help him without even realizing it. He threw up his hands and laughed. "Hello, payday!" Mother would be so proud of him when he opened his agency. Too bad Dad wasn't alive. The old man often begrudged Addy his accomplishments, but starting his own successful ad agency would have gotten the cold bastard's respect.

He flopped heavily into one of the bronze silk chairs and sipped from the flask while his heels pistoned against the pale Persian rug. Last night, he'd had a few beers before turning in. Beer seemed to put him to sleep faster than hard liquor. He'd been feeling a little tired these days, but now, now he was revved—so revved that he could barely stay still. Maker's Mark had never made him feel like this before.

He leaped up, opened the terrace door, and strode through to the sprawling expanse beyond. The late August breeze fluttered through his hair. What a view! All three rivers and the Point, not to mention the new PPG building—that black glass cathedral soaring into the sky—and the other high rises like the Gulf building mixed in with structures from earlier in the century branded the skyline unmistakably Pittsburgh. It could have been his view—would be his view in time.

He chugged a few gulps from the flask. Then he strode to the parapet and leaned against it. It was solid stone work up to his hips with a foot high crown of filigree ironwork above that. Anyone sitting in any of the terrace chairs still had a view through the ironwork.

Yeah, it'll work. A woman might stumble over the wall if she'd been drinking—or, if she'd become depressed and decided to end it all. Her mother did, so it wouldn't be too farfetched for the daughter. He swallowed more of the Maker's Mark, shook the flask, and pocketed it.

To the right, a low stone bench stood near the parapet. How convenient, especially if a shoe got left behind. He'd have to see to that. Addy sauntered to the bench.

If I'm standing on this bench when she gets here, she'll think I'm going to jump. She'll have to come out. He giggled. Then it's bye-bye, Lizzie, and hello to a cool half million!

He stepped up onto the bench. The view was even more spectacular if only because he felt like he was soaring as freely as a renegade kite. He hadn't felt this good in months. That's what really good booze could do for you.

Addy reached into his pocket for the lock pick set. Wouldn't do to have these if the law comes calling before I'm out of here. He wound up and pitched the set out so far that they landed at the end of the property in some brush at the foot of the fence at the drop off. Not bad for an out-of-practice tennis player.

He then pulled out his flask and studied it. He'd be able to afford a much classier one than the old worn thing in his hand. Anyway, he needed to be clearheaded and steady when Liz got home. Addy giggled and lobbed the flask where he'd flung the picks. He came close to tumbling over the parapet himself.

Whoa! Careful, Addy-boy!

He glanced down five tall stories at all the rocks along the flagstone path. His heart raced and stuttered. He raised his eyes to vibrant blue sky and billowing clouds. That made him feel light headed, and he began sweating.

What's happening?

His ears started buzzing, and his stomach felt like it was coming up through his throat. The buzzing got louder when Addy suddenly registered a thump of pain in the center of his back that crawled to his chest.

"Who—?" No, she wouldn't! "Liz! What are—?"

Before he could turn back to see who was there, he toppled over the parapet, banging his legs and losing a shoe.

Darkness claimed him before his body crashed onto the rocks.

§≈≈§

Liz's cab glided to the entrance of The Lafayette where two squad cars, a gray Crown Victoria sedan, and a white van with the seal of the Pittsburgh Police Department were parked. A bald black man in shirt sleeves was rummaging around in the back of the van. She opened the door after the cab came to a stop, paid the cabbie, and rushed inside.

In the spacious entertainment room off the lobby, a silver-haired man in shirt sleeves surrounded by several uniformed officers stooped over some cases containing cameras and what she supposed was forensic equipment. He reminded her of a well-coifed Mafia don from some mob film.

He handed a boyish-looking policeman a roll of bright yellow crime scene tape. "Here, Gambini, block off the scene outside. Make sure you cover the entire area." The don frowned and glanced around at the others. "I trust the other two boys in blue are still out there guarding the scene?" The small group nodded. He then put his finger behind his ear. "What's the first thing we do when we get to the scene?"

The officers answered in unison. "Secure the scene."

"We're lucky this wasn't a high traffic area." He shook his head. "Sloppy."

The young officer walked past her on his way out the door as she started towards the desk. The concierge and a new staff member were talking to a nice-looking, tall man in a summer-weight gray suit that appeared tailored to his athletic build. The short woman with the stocky peasant build beside him wore a tan pantsuit that did little for her. The man had curly, dark brown hair, blue eyes, and a face she suspected could bloom into a very appealing grin, one that seemed to be the sole property of certain charismatic Irishmen.

Seeing these two and the other police officers reminded Liz of what an ethnic smorgasbord Pittsburgh remained with its enormous immigrant population—Irish, Italian, German, Polish, Russian, Czech, Lithuanian, Swedish, Lebanese, Greek, Jewish to name only a few. She loved growing up in this town, hearing different accents and learning about different customs. When she was a little girl, everyone had a kind word for her, and sometimes a treat from their kitchens for the fatherless, little Polish girl. It was like being part of a huge multi-cultural family. And today, in 1982, the cultural distinctions lingered. Ethnic dishes in the restaurants and ethnic slurs on the streets were common. Liz wondered how long it would be before all of these unique cultures would become vague, blended flavors in the cauldron of America. She sighed. She would grieve when it all disappeared, but for now, she would enjoy the melting pot of Pittsburgh. Despite all the opportunities that would have taken her to more prestigious cities, there was no other place she cared to be other than this city with the small town ethnic heart.

Since he seemed to be occupied with the two plainclothes officers, she decided to wait until later to ask the concierge what had happened. However, as she turned towards the elevators, he caught sight of her. "Oh, Ms. Michaels."

She turned back and headed for the desk. Distress, which rarely afflicted him, clutched his entire posture. His lips trembled. "Ms. Michaels, something terrible has happened. Your—"

"Ms. Michaels," the tall man interrupted, "I'm Detective Shannon, Pittsburgh Police Department, and this is Detective Santello." Then he looked over at the silver-haired man in the entertainment room, "Luissi, you finished in there?"

"Yep, now the medical examiner's gone, the scene's all mine." Luissi heaved a sigh as he closed one of the cases and stood up. He slung a camera over his shoulder and grabbed his jacket. "Come on, officers, grab the rest of the equipment. Oh, Santello. Card game at Mac's tomorrow night."

Santello nodded.

When Shannon turned and looked at her sadly, Liz felt as if all the air had been squeezed out of her lungs. She'd felt like this when she came home to their third-floor attic apartment to find her grandmother sitting motionless at the kitchen table. That very same feeling choked her again ten years later when she found her mother's blood on the side-walk and a policeman waiting for her on the porch as a silent ambulance departed.

"Are you all right, Ms. Michaels?" asked Santello.

She nodded at Santello, whose dark eyes seemed to accuse her of some heinous act. "Tell me what's happened," Liz blurted.

Shannon took her arm and turned her toward the enter-tainment room. "Ms. Michaels, maybe it would be best if we sat down."

Liz began to tremble, but the strength of his hand on her arm calmed her. She sat on the edge of one of the gray silk-covered chairs and placed her purse and briefcase on the mahogany cocktail table before her. The detectives pulled two similar chairs opposite her. Santello took out her note-book, and Shannon looked at Liz sadly. "Ms. Michaels, this is never easy. Your husband—"

Liz stiffened, a little confused. "My ex-husband?"

Shannon nodded. "A woman walking her dog found Mr. Payne's body along the walking path behind the building."

Liz gasped. She shook her head. "What? Addy's dead?"

"Yes."

"How?"

"The medical examiner said his injuries look like he'd sustained a fall, possibly from your terrace. We'll know more after a search of your place and the autopsy."

Liz became very still and then shook her head again. "I don't understand. How in the world could he have fallen from my terrace?"

"We're still investigating that." He adjusted his seat and looked like he'd rather be any place but here. "Are you okay to answer some questions?"

Santello squirmed in her chair and looked at Shannon like he'd grown donkey ears.

In her mind's eye, all Liz could see was a broken, blond Raggedy Andy sprawled on some rocks. She scrunched her eyes to make the image go away. Then she nodded.

He cleared his throat. "When was the last time you saw Mr. Payne?" he asked.

"Two days ago."

"Here?"

"No, my office. I don't allow him here."

"Would you mind telling us why he visited you?"

"He wanted to borrow money for a business venture."

Shannon raised his head. His eyes no longer showed concern. Santello looked at him with the flicker of a sneer and began jotting in her notebook.

"And did you agree to lend him the money?" Shannon said.

"No. I told him to get a job."

Santello stopped writing. A glimmer of amusement peeked from her eyes, but then she bowed her head back to her notes.

"Can you think of any reason why he would be in your apartment?" continued Shannon.

She shrugged and shook her head. "I don't know. Maybe he thought I'd be more receptive if he talked to me here. No audience." Liz looked out at the concierge desk in the lobby. "I can't imagine how he got in. No, he couldn't have gotten into my place." She remembered their last meeting and began to tear up. "Do you think he could have jumped from the roof?"

"What makes you think that?" Santello asked.

Liz barely held back her tears. "Addy was a very successful advertising executive, but over the last few years, everything's been a downhill slide for him. He always drank too much, but his drinking had gotten a lot worse. He was a very proud man." She considered a moment and then looked at Shannon, who seemed the friendlier of the two. "Do you think if I'd given him the money, he'd still be alive?" Tears spilled down her face. Liz swallowed and felt something hard and cold lodge in the pit of her being. "Why did he do it here?"

"Ms. Michaels, the nature of Mr. Payne's death hasn't been determined yet. It could have been an accident or possibly homicide," Shannon said.

"Homi—"

"You said you didn't allow him here? Has he ever been in your place?" Santello said.

"No. Never."

"Uh-huh." Santello jotted in her notebook. "We'll need the names of people who can vouch for your whereabouts today."

"My whereabouts! Surely you don't think—"

"It's standard procedure. Process of elimination." Santello said. "Where were you today?"

"At work. Then I had lunch with my friend, Miriam Kernan, and was back in the office until around five thirty or so."

Santello stared at her with blank eyes and shoved the notebook and pen at her. "Please write down her contact information and your place of employment. Also list anyone else who may have seen you this afternoon."

"And if there is anyone else we should contact about Mr. Payne," added Shannon.

"That would be his mother. Eunice Payne. She lives in Cleveland. Shaker Heights. This is really going to hit her hard. Addy is her golden boy." She sighed. "You should know, one way or another, she'll make it my fault. Please don't tell her I refused to give him a loan." Then Liz laughed. "Actually, she wouldn't believe Addy asked me for a loan. I'm sure he kept his circumstances a secret from her."

Santello lifted her eyebrows and looked at Shannon. He returned her stare. "I see no reason to go into detail about his meeting with you," he said.

Liz jotted down the information and handed the notebook and pen back to Santello.

"With your permission, we'll have Forensics check your place when they're finished outside," Shannon said.

"He can't have fallen from my terrace, Detectives. The Kernans, who are the closest thing I have to family, and the concierge staff are the only people who have keys. They would never give Addy a key, and the staff has a strict policy of recording every time they unlock an apartment along with the reason for opening it. Besides, every guest not accompanied by an owner must sign in at the desk. There's no way Addy was in my place."

"How about when the desk is unmanned?" Santello said.

"The lobby doors are locked, and only the residents have keys to them. The doors are set to lock automatically after a resident enters."

Shannon nodded. "Still, he could have sneaked in somehow. He could have walked in with one of the other residents. A system like that is prone to human error, and there are things besides keys that can open a lock, Ms. Michaels."

Closing her notebook, Santello smirked. "Or maybe you let him in?"

Liz frowned.

Shannon raised an eyebrow at Santello, but she didn't look like she noticed.

"So, do we have your permission to check your place, or do we have to get a search warrant?" she said.

"Yes, yes! I have nothing to hide."

"Good. Do you have somewhere you can stay in the meantime?" Shannon said.

"Why?"

"You won't be able to stay here until we're finished with it. We need to keep it free of contamination," Santello said.

"What! For how long?"

Santello smiled faintly. "As long as it takes."

Shannon glared at Santello and added, "It will probably only be a few days."

"What about my clothes?"

"I'll go with you up to your place so you can pack whatever you need. If you have to use the bathroom, you can use the ladies room down here." Santello said.

"But my toothbrush! My toiletries!"

Santello smiled, but the smile never made it to her eyes. "You can buy whatever you need in the meantime."

Liz thought about the salmon filet and the vegetables in her refrigerator. She straightened her shoulders. "I have food that needs to be cooked. Any problem with my taking it with me?"

Santello shook her head. "Sorry. No can do."

Liz squinted at the woman and clenched her teeth.

"If you need to call anyone, use the phone down here at the desk. . . . Oh, and we'll need to fingerprint you."

Liz stared at her, open-mouthed.

"It's so we can eliminate your prints from any others we find in your place. Standard procedure." Shannon said.

After being fingerprinted by the black forensic tech, Liz called Miriam from the phone at the desk. She could no longer contain her anger as she related how Addy had again complicated her life and how the police were treating her. Miriam listened quietly.

"You shouldn't be driving. Gerald is back from New York. He'll pick you up and take you to the drugstore so you can buy anything you need. We will have dinner when you get here. Oh, and it would be best if you waited outside for him, away from those detectives. You know how he gets. He might have a few choice words for that Detective Santello."

Liz smiled. "I think I would enjoy seeing that, but you're right. He doesn't need to have his blood pressure skyrocket."

"And he doesn't need to get into a shoving match with a police officer. . . . You know, it will be like old times when you lived with us, *Liebling*. You can have your old room."

Neither Liz nor Santello spoke during the time it took the elevator to reach the fifth floor. Santello occasionally eyed her. Liz didn't like the look on her face. She sighed and straightened her jacket.

A policeman was stationed in the hall in front of her double doors. He nodded at Santello and stepped aside. Black dust clung to the doorknobs as well as the rosewood doors. She opened the doors and felt revenged when Santello's mouth dropped at the view like hers had when she first saw it.

Take that, Dragon Lady!

Then Santello stared long and hard at the floors and steps.

What's she looking for?

The woman looked up at her. "Let's get you packed."

In the bedroom, Liz very deliberately took out one item at a time, slowly folded it, and then placed it in the suitcase— the biggest one she owned.

Santello, stone-faced, arms crossed, looked around the room—at the ivory walls and drapes, the thick ivory carpeting, the pale blue brocade bedding, the copies of works by the Impressionists and some more recent artist originals, the ornate antique furniture, the deep walk-in closet, and oversized en suite bath. Her tight mouth and glittering eyes did not escape Liz.

"You done, yet?"

"Almost," Liz crossed back to the dresser for the fifth time and allowed herself a self-satisfied grin.

ᏋᎵᏋSIXᏋᏋ

MARCO SNEERED AT the two detectives who parked their Crown Vic in front of the gray sandstone station—so full of themselves with their talk and jokes. They wouldn't be laughing for long. He'd see to that.

He strolled down the cracked sidewalk to an old, red Pontiac GTO. When he glanced back at them, the two cops were still focused on each other and never turned around when the door of The Judge creaked. His older brother had affectionately named the muscle car that because it got a lot of respect from their crowd. Marco felt like James Bond when his brother allowed him to drive it to the senior prom. It really impressed his date, enough so that he'd scored. Now that Tony was dead, it was no longer on loan until his release; The Judge was his.

He owed Tony.

After the two detectives bounded up the worn stone steps and pushed through the doors of the station, he drove away to plan the payback for his dead brother.

꿏

"Awfully quiet for an Irishman, Shannon," Santello said. "She got to you, didn't she?"

Shannon gave her the fish eye as he got out of the car and then looked away. Yeah, those incredible ocean eyes; you could almost see the waves crashing. A man could drown in eyes like that—large irises tinged with black around the edge.

They bounded up the steps, and Santello paged through her notebook before putting it into her huge shoulder bag. "Well, what's your take on this case?"

They pressed through the doors and headed to the squad room. "Let's see what Forensics comes up with. I'd like to talk to Squires after he's done the autopsy, too." He looked down at her from his six foot two height with a slight grin. "Then I'll give you my take. Otherwise, I know what you'll say if I tell you what I think now."

"Hey, sport, she may be skinny, she may be rich, she may be pretty, but she killed him. And those crocodile tears? Oh, yeah, she's guilty all right."

The spoor of scorched coffee, cigarettes, and the discarded remains of lunch signaled they'd reached the squad room even before they opened the door. Korpielsky, another detective, was still there, pulling some overtime like them.

"I've seen that look on the faces of the family of suicides a hundred times." Shannon said.

She shook her head and raised her eyes to the ceiling. "Whatever you say, Seamus Aloysius." She only used his given name when she was absolutely sure he was clueless.

When they sat across from each other at their scarred wooden desks, Korpielsky shuffled his long skinny frame over to them. "Did you hear about that perp Cantuso you got last year?" he said.

"What, he's out on parole already?" Santello said.

Korpielsky lifted his shaggy black brows. "No, he got a taste of his own medicine. Somebody at the prison beat him to death."

Shannon glanced at Santello.

She held his glance. "Can't say that I'm sorry. He was one mean bully. Should've gotten more than manslaughter."

Shannon frowned and shook his head.

"What?"

"Listen to us. Happy someone's dead."

"Aw, Shannon."

"Yeah, I know, he was scum. Still—"

"Enough, Shannon. The pregnant wife of the guy he beat to death didn't know it was her husband's body until she saw the birthmark on his shoulder. Ever wonder how she and the baby are doing?"

"I know how they're doing. Probably better than if the husband were still around. They got a lot of help from family and other sources."

Santello raised an eyebrow. "Other sources, huh?"

Korpielsky waited for Shannon to elaborate. Shannon's eyes warned Santello to button up. She knew what the other sources were. He'd sworn her to secrecy sometime ago when she found out he'd set up a private foundation with some of his inheritance to help out a few of the victims they came across. Aside from a paid up mortgage on a modest duplex and a mother who didn't have to work because of a monthly check, Shannon made sure that baby had a college trust fund.

Santello eyed Korpielsky. "Okay, enough said."

Korpielsky sighed, grabbed his jacket, and headed out. "See you guys tomorrow."

"Want to toss for who gets to notify Payne's mother?" Santello said.

Shannon won the toss. He hated notifying next of kin by phone. He was relieved when no one at Eunice Payne's residence answered. He thought about calling the police department in Shaker Heights to ask them to make a personal visit. However, though it wouldn't be as useful as seeing the woman in person, talking to her on the phone himself might give him information that could lead to closing the case. Even over the phone, tone and language revealed much. Besides, he was intrigued by what Liz Michael's said about her former mother-in-law. Must be quite a history there. He would try again later.

After about half an hour of plowing through the never-ending paperwork, Santello pitched a stack of papers into their out box and stared at Shannon until he looked up. "That Liz Michaels." She shook her head and scowled. "The guy fell from her terrace, Shannon. Luissi said his prints were on the doors, and they found his shoe near the parapet. That proves he was there. And Luissi didn't find a key for her place on him, not even a lock pick. She's in this somehow."

Shannon shook his head. He knew that once Santello sank her teeth into a theory, she wouldn't let it go until she could prove it, or it turned out baseless. He came up with the safest response he could think of. "She said she was at work. Lots of people probably saw her."

"We still have to check that out. Even so, she could have hired someone to off him—maybe a woman—and had her pass herself off as the cleaning lady. Or maybe one of the neighbors did it for her."

Shannon stopped writing, sat back in his chair, and narrowed his eyes at her. "There wasn't anyone signed in, and remember, the concierge said this wasn't the cleaning woman's day. They hadn't let anyone else into her place either. And you saw the neighbors who were home when it happened—even if any of them looked on her as a long-lost daughter, which one of those Golden Oldies could have done it?"

Santello shrugged.

"Those ladies are more concerned about the rocks on their fingers and the rhinestone collars on their lap dogs. They could not care less about what's going on in their young neighbor's life." He leaned forward. "Santello, why are you so set on pinning this on her?"

She regarded him with a set mouth and raised eyebrows. "Shannon, I saw how you were with her."

"What do you mean 'how I was with her'?"

"Are you okay to answer some questions?"

"What? She just heard that her husband was dead."

"Her ex-husband. Shannon, these la-de-da rich types are so used to being catered to, they think they can get away with anything. Humph, not like my family. Hell, all of us worked from the time we could wash a dish. And no way could we steal even a pencil without paying big time." She tapped her chest. "I'm the first in my family to go to college. Paid my own way."

Shannon nodded. "I know. And you have every right to be proud of yourself."

Santello huffed. "She had motive, and I'll bet she had opportunity." Then she stopped and grinned. "She had balls, though, to tell him to get a job. I kinda liked that."

Shannon smiled. "You sure that's not all you liked? I've seen you badmouth women you were attracted to before."

Santello snorted. "Ha!"

He looked at her sadly, recalling how much torment she'd suffered nursing her partner through Stage Four cancer. "She does remind me a little of Mona."

Santello narrowed her eyes. "Mona and that woman are nothing alike!"

"I'm just saying—" but the look on her face cut him off, and he buried his head in the file in front of him.

Santello grabbed her bag and left without a word. Her crepe soles whispered her irritation at him down the hall.

ꞗ⁊SEVEN⁊ꞗ

SHANNON STRETCHED OUT his long legs and rubbed the crick out of his neck. Time to head home. Following up on Michaels would best be done tomorrow when all the city offices would be open. Before he could leave, though, he had to try Payne's mother again. Eunice Payne might know why her son was at Michaels' place.

Hm, Liz Michaels? She would be too smart to kill him or have him killed at her apartment, although he'd been a detective long enough to know anything was possible. Still, he kept seeing her face, those eyes, and her distress at Payne's death. She had the cool demeanor of a businesswoman—obviously a successful one—and yet, something in her eyes, her guilt over not lending Payne the money, told him her life had not been a straight path to success from birth. If Payne's mother disliked Michaels so much, it could have something to do with her background. On the other hand, Mrs. Payne may have seen a more sinister aspect of Liz Michaels the woman was clever enough to mask.

He sighed. And Santello, as much as he hated to admit it, was often right. She was savvy, tough, and respected. She'd earned her bars the hard way years ago when she took two bullets protecting her partner and made an arrest despite her wounds.

Shannon sipped his cold coffee and grimaced. The mouthwatering aroma of hot homemade dinners and restaurant fare some of the detectives were eating at their desks provoked a long, sonorous growl from his stomach. A few of them looked at him and grinned. He picked up the phone and punched in Mrs. Payne's number. It rang several times before being picked up.

"Payne residence," a woman's voice answered.

"This is Detective Shannon from the Pittsburgh Police Department. May I speak to Mrs. Payne?"

"Mrs. Payne is out for the evening. I'm Adelaide Hauser, her housekeeper. What is this about, Detective?"

"I'd rather speak with Mrs. Payne personally. Will she be in tomorrow afternoon?"

"I believe so. I see nothing on her calendar."

So, he'd be able to meet the woman face to face after all. "Would you tell Mrs. Payne that I will be there around 2:00— if it's convenient?" He rattled off his direct number for the housekeeper in case Mrs. Payne could not meet with him.

"She'll want to know what this is about. What should I tell her?"

"Just tell her it's a police matter that I must discuss with her in private." That should keep the housekeeper from asking for more information. It didn't seem right that the house-keeper should know about Payne's death before his mother did.

After ending the call, Shannon sat a moment. The drive to Shaker Heights ruled out his researching Michaels. Santello would have to do it. He smirked. She'd relish digging up any dirt she could find in Liz Michael's past. He hoped the woman had a clean record.

He shrugged into his jacket and strode down the corridor. There were other nights when leaving the job meant going home to Angie, his warm, cuddly Italian wife. The image of her big with child, her dark curls framing a glowing face that lit up like the sun when he came home, often visited him at times like this. Sitting in the driver's seat of his Buick Regal, he looked over at the passenger seat she would never cozy into again. It didn't seem like it had already been three years since that awful night he'd lost both her and the baby. Eclampsia, the doctor called it—a nice scientific name for an event that gouged his heart out. The doctor had detected the pre-eclampsia symptoms early in her pregnancy and scheduled an early delivery to avoid complications, but it all went wrong.

Following the funeral, his sister, Eileen, had insisted he move in with them. Her husband had died a few years earlier. She said that living with them would be best for everyone, especially his nephew. So he scotched the grand house plans Angie and he had made and moved out of their spacious apartment. No Angie, no baby—no need for the dream house that would have housed many little Shannons to come.

Shannon pulled into the driveway of his sister's Tudor house in Rosslyn Farms. Ivy had done well in the insurance business, which was good considering they had four children, and Ivy was too proud to allow Eileen to use her inheritance. His three nieces were out of the house now, and Paddy was the youngest, a family position they shared since Shannon had also been the youngest of five. Eileen was the oldest of Shannon's four sisters, often assuming the mother role, especially after their parents died. He could sympathize with Paddy, knowing what it had been like to be the baby brother. They both had been spoiled, but they also had been the brunt of their respective sisters' pranks and rare bad temper.

Before he could open the door, Paddy opened it for him. Excitement brightened his face. "I didn't think you'd ever get here. Mom put some dinner aside for you in the oven "

Shannon smiled at the eagerness in his twenty-year-old nephew's face, realizing how important it was for him to have a male ear to share whatever accomplishment he'd achieved that day. Sometimes he seemed younger than he really was. It saddened him that Ivy wasn't here to see his son growing into this passionate, talented young man.

He followed Paddy to the family-sized kitchen, warm and inviting with its white cabinets, blue gingham curtains, and delft blue tiles depicting windmills and farms. An oak wall clock marked the time, and the scent of roast beef still lingered. The cackling and laughter of women drifted through the closed doors of the living room into the kitchen.

"Sit, Uncle Jim. I'll get your dinner." Paddy opened the refrigerator. "What do you want to drink? Not coffee. How about a beer?"

"Milk sounds better." Shannon eased into the solid oak chair of the dining set that had belonged to his parents.

"What are your mom and sisters cooking up in the living room?"

"They're helping Maura plan her showing at Mossman's Gallery next week."

"All of them?"

"Like always."

"And they didn't include you?"

Paddy removed lids from still-hot casserole pans; loaded a plate with roast beef, roasted potatoes, carrots, and peas; and placed it before Shannon.

"Oh, they'll use me for the heavy lifting."

After pouring a glass of chilled milk for him and one for himself, Paddy sat down and leaned his elbows on the table, waiting for Shannon to eat. Out of the corner of his eye, Shannon watched him finally take a sip of milk. Paddy's foot syncopated under the table as Shannon rapidly forked his dinner down.

"So, anything special happen today?"

Paddy grinned and, like a racehorse released from the gate, sprinted into his news. "I think I've got a great shot at getting that internship."

Shannon's eyes widened. "Yeah?"

"They want to see some of my writing, even if I don't get the internship."

"Seems to me you have an internship if they want to see your writing. Uh, any dinner rolls left?"

Paddy grimaced and shook his head. "No, Maura and I finished them off."

Shannon returned to the rest of his dinner. "So, how many internships are there?"

"Three."

"What will you be doing?"

"They usually start interns out with office stuff like filing and running errands, but you get to see what the staff is doing and how the place is run. If they think you can handle it, they let you prescreen submissions."

"Well, I think you're in." Shannon stood. "You know, your dad would be very proud of you."

Paddy looked away and then nodded. Female laughter again chimed from the living room.

"When will you know?" Shannon took his plate to the stove and served himself more beef and potatoes.

"Probably in a week. The secretary let me know that they were interviewing fifteen candidates."

Shannon took his seat, dabbed at a spot of gravy on his chin, and smiled at him. "You going to last that long without exploding?"

Paddy looked at him in exasperation. "Uncle Jim, I'm not a kid anymore!"

Shannon nodded as he forked the savory beef into his mouth.

"So how was your day?" Paddy asked.

Shannon looked at him and shook his head. He didn't want to relive his work day—not any work day. The battered woman they'd found in the alley that morning, then Payne in the afternoon, not to mention the emaciated infant discovered during a drug raid last week had him thinking again that maybe he should leave the job before the job reamed him into an unfeeling shell. A man could take only so much evil.

The doors of the living room opened, and Eileen and her daughters, eyes sparkling, spilled into the foyer. When they saw Shannon, his nieces swarmed him with hugs. The oldest was the first to make her goodbyes. Eileen and her daughters hugged each other and promised to be in touch the following day. After his nieces left, the house felt a little less alive to Shannon. He saw it reflected in his sister's and nephew's eyes as well. People die. People leave. But unlike Angie and Ivy, his nieces would return.

⚔EIGHT⚔

SHANNON PULLED THE unmarked, gray Crown Vic around the circular drive and parked in front of Mrs. Payne's stately, three-story, dark-red brick residence. White columns supported a portico over the double oak doors, and floor to ceiling windows graced the front of the home on either side of the portico. Like the other properties in this area, it was a statement of dignity and old money.

He was not impressed. Although Shannon's family had lived modestly in comparison, their father's trucking company took them to many functions at the far grander homes of business associates. Besides, Shannon and his four sisters had each inherited a trust that could afford them a more ostentatious lifestyle, but they chose instead to shepherd the wealth for future generations as well as lend a hand to the deserving. This was the Shannon way according to their late father.

Shannon mounted the short flight of steps to the doors and used one of the heavy, carved brass knockers centered on each door. The sound echoed briefly before he noticed the doorbell. He waited a few minutes, and when no one answered, he rang the bell. A melody of muffled delicate chimes floated through the heavy doors. Shortly, one of the doors opened.

A stout, gray-haired, plain woman in a simple navy dress regarded him a moment. "Yes?"

Shannon presented his identification. "I'm Detective Shannon. Mrs. Payne?"

"*Miss* Hauser. Come in, Detective. Mrs. Payne is expecting you."

She led him to a sitting room painted and papered in pale mint green and furnished with antiques, including the rose silk camelback settee where she indicated he could sit. The trace of jasmine and rose underscored by lemon furniture polish would have been an intrusion in any other setting. He looked back at the broad foyer where the dark green-carpeted staircase bisected the generous space like the wide stem of a lush climbing vine. The chandelier was not the largest he'd ever seen, but it was definitely good quality and sparkled as though it had never been touched by anything as common as dust.

Miss Hauser hung up the house phone. "Mrs. Payne knows you're here. She'll be with you shortly. Would you like something to drink? Coffee, tea, a soft drink?"

"Thank you. I'm fine."

"If you'll excuse me then?"

Shannon nodded, and Miss Hauser disappeared down a hall beyond the foyer. Almost immediately, a lithe older woman with a perfect, blond pageboy appeared at the top of the stairs. She wore a brief, white, flirty-skirted tennis outfit and paused a moment, as if allowing him to appreciate what he saw.

Eunice Payne then bounced lightly down the stairs. "Detective Shannon, you must excuse me. I'd planned to change before you got here, but I was running late. Had lunch with a dear friend of mine after my match at the club and just couldn't get away. She doesn't get to Shaker Heights often since her husband became governor." Her voice was resonant and strong for someone her size, and she clearly loved the sound of it.

Shannon stood. "That's quite all right."

She reached the bottom of the stairs, and as she came toward him, the fine lines and creases around her pale blue eyes and red-lipsticked mouth clearly showed.

"Come. The den is far more comfortable than the salon."

Shannon trailed her across the cream marble foyer to a door that opened to a distinctively male office. Perhaps it had been her late husband's. Money green—that's what Angie would have called the color on the walls. There was plenty of room for a huge ornately-carved mahogany desk, a wall of bookcases behind it, and a sitting area with a tobacco leather sofa and a couple of well-used armchairs. Brass lamps with cream silk shades sat on the desk and lamp tables. Shannon could almost smell the whiskey and cigars.

Eunice relaxed onto one end of the sofa, showing her petite figure to its best advantage. Shannon sat in one of the armchairs and perched on the edge of the seat.

"So, Detective, what is a policeman from Pittsburgh doing in Ohio?" She sat up and brightened. "Ah, you must be here about my former daughter-in-law. I'm not surprised. I knew it would only be a matter of time before she did something that would land her in trouble." She relaxed back into the embrace of the sofa with a smug smile.

"No, Mrs. Payne. I'm not here about Ms. Michaels."

She lost her smile. "Oh?"

"Mrs. Payne, I'm sorry to have to inform you that your son met with an accident yesterday afternoon."

She sat up straight. "An accident?" Her voice became strident. "Why didn't he call me? Is he unconscious? In a coma?" Her face hardened. "He can't be in jail."

Shannon's silence told her what no mother wants to hear. She wilted like a water-starved bloom. "No. . . ."

"I'm sorry, Mrs. Payne. He died yesterday afternoon."

Eunice stared at Shannon like a stopped clock. Then her face crumpled, "He's dead? My Addy's dead?"

"Would you like me to call someone for you?"

"You say he had an accident?" she asked through her tears. "Damn that sports car! I never liked that thing."

"No, it wasn't a car accident, Mrs. Payne. Your son fell to his death."

Eunice looked at him a moment, her wet face gray, older. "What? How? Please . . . tell me how he died."

"We believe he fell from the terrace of Ms. Michael's apartment. He was found on the path of the grounds beneath her unit."

She regarded him stonily. "That know-nothing. That fraud! She killed him!"

Eunice rose and paced back and forth. "She couldn't stand that he was so much more talented, so much more successful!"

She spun around and stalked toward him, her face red, her eyes glaring. "You know, her mother died from a fall. . . . Have you arrested her?"

Shannon shook his head.

Eunice appeared genuinely stunned. "Why not?" Her voice echoed beyond the den.

Before Shannon could answer, Miss Hauser rushed in. "Mrs. Payne, what's wrong?"

Eunice stared at her housekeeper as though the woman were a puzzle piece that simply did not fit and then collapsed. "It's Addy. That low-born trash, Michaels, killed him!"

"What!" Miss Hauser looked at Shannon with the dark, beady eyes of a raven.

Shannon sprang up to help Eunice. "We have no evidence that Miss Michaels was involved. We are still investigating why he was at her home and how it happened."

"Oh, she did it, all right!" Eunice said through clenched teeth.

They lifted Eunice from the floor and sat her in an armchair. "Mrs. Payne, please, you must calm down. Remember your blood pressure." Miss Hauser said.

Eunice shook her head and burst into tears again.

"Detective, would you please stay. I must call her doctor."

"Of course."

Oh, boy, this case! Talk about walking on eggshells. He regarded the distraught woman. Could this woman have good reason for accusing Liz Michaels of killing her son? He recalled blue eyes a man could drown in. Shannon hoped not and then chastised himself. He had to maintain his objectivity no matter where the case went.

Maybe it really is time to get out of police work.

❧NINE❧

SANTELLO CONTEMPLATED THE mature, dark-haired woman in the tailored ivory suit. She caught a whiff of—Chanel No. 5? Shalimar? Santello had tried both scents, but they wound up smelling like wet cardboard on her. The office furnishings were antique—and commanding. However, the brown, rust, burgundy, gold, and navy in the fabrics and carpeting warmed the effect. Miriam Kernan's dark-brown eyes—eyes that could reign over an armada—regarded her calmly.

Oh, yeah, she's one tough cookie alright. Wonder what made her that way?

"Of course, I'll be happy to answer any questions you have, Detective."

Santello nodded. "I appreciate that, Mrs. Kernan." She rifled through her notebook, flipping to a blank page. "You had lunch with Ms. Michaels yesterday?"

"Yes, we went to Vinaigrette."

"What time was that?"

"A little after noon."

"And what time did you finish?"

Miriam toyed with a gold pen. "Oh, it was nearly one thirty."

Santello looked up from her notes after entering the information. "You left together?"

Miriam stared at her a moment. "No. No, I had some business to take care of across town before returning to work."

"Uh huh. . . . So, when did you get back to the office?"

"Around three thirty—four."

"Uh-huh. . . . Was Ms. Michaels in her office?"

Miriam frowned. "Why wouldn't she be?"

Santello paused a moment, looked down at her notes, and then looked hard at Miriam. "I'm asking if you saw her back at the office."

Miriam pursed her lips and hesitated. "I didn't actually see her. When Ms. Michaels is busy, she often closes her blinds, locks her door, and unplugs her phone."

"I notice you have another door in your office. Where does it lead?"

"To a hallway."

"And that goes where?"

"To the restrooms and the lobby."

"And to a stairwell?"

"Yes, at the other end."

"And does Ms. Michael's office have a door to that hallway, too?"

"Yes."

"So, her blinds were down, and the door was locked?"

"Yes, her blinds were down. I presume her door was locked and her phone unplugged. You can ask her assistant."

Santello closed her notebook, checked her watch and stood. "I'd like to talk to her if she's still here."

"I'm sure she is." Miriam pressed the intercom buttons.

"Mandy, I have a Detective Santello here who wants to ask you some questions. Would you please meet her in the conference room?"

The line was silent.

"Mandy?"

"Uh, yeah, sure. . . . Now?"

Miriam smiled at the detective. "The sooner, the better."

"Sure, Mrs. Kernan. I-I'm on my way."

Miriam rose from her desk, tall in heels that transformed her slender five-foot-three frame to a commanding five foot six.

Santello eyed the woman again. Only a tidal wave could topple this gal, but where was Mrs. Kernan yesterday afternoon?

Miriam continued smiling but her eyes were now cool. "Martha, my assistant, will escort you to the conference room, Detective."

Santello stood and crossed to the door. She paused a moment, her hand on the door knob, before she turned back to Miriam. "By the way, Mrs. Kernan, where did you go after lunch with Ms. Michaels?"

The smile disappeared from Miriam's face, and her eyes looked ready to command a siege. Santello waited.

"I had some personal business to take care of. If I need an alibi, Detective, there are people who can verify my whereabouts—but I'd rather not provide that information at the moment."

Hm? Not the type for a little afternoon delight. Medical tests? Maybe that's what she wants me to think. . . . No. Tough broad, but not a killer. Wouldn't dirty her hands. Santello nodded once and opened the door. "Thank you for your time, Mrs. Kernan."

Santello nearly collided with Liz on her way out. They looked at each other like gunslingers ready to draw. Liz spoke first. "When will I be able to move back into my home? Surely, you've found everything you could possibly find by now."

"Well, I'll check with Forensics and let you know."

Santello had the look of an athlete who'd scored the winning point. Oh yeah, it's payback time, honey. You don't make Rose Santello wait while you take your good old time packing. She pressed by Liz and glanced back with a smirk. "You'll know as soon as I do."

ᏨᎥᎥ**TEN**ᎥᎥᏨ

SHANNON AMBLED INTO the squad room and stopped when he heard Santello on the phone.

"Yeah, don't take the tape down at Michaels' place. I'll let you know when we're finished with it."

Santello ended the call, hunched over the papers on her desk, and tapped her pen—usually a sign she was juggling theories. She glanced up when he came around and plopped his notebook on his desk. "So, how'd the interview with the mother go?"

Shannon decided not to make an issue of her call to Forensics. He removed his jacket and loosened his tie before parking himself at the desk across from her. "You know that movie, *Sunset Boulevard*?"

"Yeah, Gloria Swanson playing some old actress trying to look young."

"Well, Mrs. Payne could give that old actress a run for her money."

"Yeah?"

"Yeah, and she's convinced Michaels killed her son."

"Uh-huh. . . . Did she say why?"

"She thinks Michaels was jealous of him."

Santello snickered. "More like Michaels was fed up with him hitting her up for money."

"So how did your day go?"

Santello scratched her cheek and ran her fingers through her hair. "I think we got to take a closer look at Michaels. Everyone I talked to thinks she was in her office, but no one could say they actually saw her yesterday afternoon. The receptionist thought she saw her come in but wasn't certain because she was on the phone. Mrs. Kernan—now talk about movies, she'd have been a great Queen Elizabeth. Reminds me of that old black and white movie used to come on TV when I was a kid. Who played her? Betty Davis?"

Shannon shrugged and shook his head.

Santello snorted. "Anyway, they had lunch together, but Kernan went off on her own and didn't get back to the company until around three thirty or four. She assumed Michaels was in her office. Michael's assistant didn't see her come in, but thought Michaels was in her office because her phone was off, and the blinds were down."

Shannon looked puzzled. "So what makes her think Michaels was in her office?"

"That's her routine when she wants to work without interruption. Oh, and I noticed Mrs. Kernan had another door in her office. She said it opened to a hallway that led to a stairwell. Michaels has the same set up."

"So she can come and go without anyone knowing?"

Santello nodded and raised her eyebrows at Shannon.

"What did the concierge at her co-op say when you interviewed him?"

Santello smiled and shook her head. "You know, for what those people pay, they should have better security. The concierge said he recognized everyone who came in and didn't see Michaels until the end of the day when we were there. His assistant said there were a bunch of women who came in when the concierge was at lunch. He didn't think any of them looked like Michaels, but he's new on the job."

"Hm. . . . You said Mrs. Kernan went off on her own and didn't get back to her office until close to four? Where was she?"

"On personal business, and she didn't want to talk about it. You should see those eyes. Anyway, she says she's got witnesses."

Shannon drummed his fingers on the desk, pensive. "Let's schedule an interview with Michaels tomorrow—at her office. I'd like to get a look at it."

Shannon slid into one of the chairs before Liz's desk and noticed how different her office was from the apartment he'd inspected the day of Payne's death. With its sage-colored walls, the spacious office was well appointed and sleek. Her simple Brazilian rosewood desk was clear except for a gold pen, leather-encased appointment book, phone, and a single yellow pad off to the side. The rest of the furniture matched the desk. No carpeting covered the dark-stained wood floors.

A palm plant by the windows nearly touched the ceiling. The wood blinds were open, but the temperature remained cool despite the August heat. Awards crowded one wall, some as early as 1975 and a few as recent as last year. The only resemblance to her elegant apartment was an ornately-framed print on the opposite wall of an Impressionist painting. A pleasant floral scent—probably her perfume—wafted lightly through the air.

Santello took her seat beside him as he pulled out his notebook and pen. Shannon smiled. "Thank you for making time for us today."

Liz did not return his smile. "You happened to catch me at a good time, Detectives," She reached toward the intercom button. "Would you like some coffee or tea?"

Both Santello and Shannon shook their heads. "Thanks, no. We have a few questions for you if you don't mind," he said. "Then we'll be on our way."

Liz folded her hands on her desk. "And if I do mind?"

Shannon shrugged his shoulders and cocked his head to one side.

"We can talk here, or we can escort you to the station. It's all the same to us," Santello said.

Liz grimaced and settled back in her chair. "What do you want to know?"

"Where were you between the time of your lunch with Mrs. Kernan and the time you arrived at your home the day of Mr. Payne's death?" Shannon said.

She looked at them like the question made no sense. "I was right here."

"In your office?" Santello said.

Liz nodded and tapped her desk. "Right here."

"The whole time?" Santello said.

"Yes. We're negotiating a contract to buy another publishing company, and I had stacks of manuscripts that needed my attention. We were in a time crunch, so all of it had to be done that day."

Shannon nodded and wrote in his notebook. "Did anyone see you during that time?"

"I don't know. I doubt it. I close my blinds, lock the door, and unplug the phone when I'm swamped."

Santello gestured to the door that led to the hallway. "And when you left, you used that door?"

"Yes. I often have a cab meet me on that side of the building. Traffic is lighter there."

"And you use the same cab company all the time?" she continued.

"Yes, Ace Taxi."

Santello nodded and glanced at Shannon.

"Detectives, what's going on here? Is there something odd about Addy's death?"

"We won't know the cause of his death until the coroner makes his report. We're just following up on a few details," Shannon said. He smiled at her briefly, closed his notebook, and stood. Santello followed suit.

As they reached the door, Santello stopped and turned to Liz. "Oh, by the way, do you know where Mrs. Kernan might have gone after lunch?"

"What?" Liz's eyes sparked. "Perhaps you should ask Mrs. Kernan herself."

Santello nodded.

"Thank you very much, Ms. Michaels." Shannon returned to her desk and held out his card. "If you think of anything that might be helpful, here's my card."

Liz did not reach for the card, so Shannon placed it in the middle of her desk with a brief smile.

Liz's eyes narrowed. "By the way, Detective Santello, did you find out when I'll be able to move back to my place?"

"Well, Forensics is supposed to call me back about that."

Shannon caught Santello's eye and stifled a smile. He turned to Liz. "If I may use your phone, I'll check with Forensics right now."

Santello gave him a killing look.

Liz handed him the receiver and crossed her arms. "Be my guest."

He noticed how slender her hands were when he took the phone from her and punched in the number. "Hi, Luissi. Shannon here. Say, are you finished with the Michaels place? . . . Uh-huh." Shannon eyed Santello, but she looked away and studied the awards on the wall.

Liz raised an eyebrow.

"No, no, we're done with it. . . . Gotcha. Good." He handed the receiver back to Liz. "You can go home tonight."

Liz nodded curtly.

As they made their way through the lobby, Santello ignored Shannon's smirk and strode ahead of him. "I'll check with Ace Taxi to see if she used them earlier in the day."

"Check the other companies, too." Shannon couldn't help smiling at her discomfort.

At the elevators, Santello grimaced. "You know, she could have taken a quick bus ride and then the Mt. Washington Incline."

Shannon pushed the button for the elevator. "Would she have had time?"

"We'll find out. Wonder when Squires will have that report for us?"

⟨ELEVEN⟩

LIZ TAPPED SHANNON'S card on her desk and then grabbed it between both hands ready to tear it to shreds. Instead, she slapped it on the desk. What she really wanted to do was smack that Detective Santello. She shot up from her chair, launching it several feet behind her into the palm tree.

How dare that woman keep me out of my home for no good reason! If I didn't have better things to do, I'd call their superior and complain!

Liz retrieved her chair and pushed it up to her desk. And how dare they insinuate that Miriam had anything to do with Addy's death! She paced her office. It's one thing to think I had something to do with it—no, it's ridiculous to even think that I had anything to do with it! If they knew how my mother died. . . . And Miriam could never harm another human being.

Liz tore out of her office, startling Mandy, and headed for Miriam's office. Miriam's assistant was nowhere in sight. Liz tapped quickly before entering.

Miriam looked up from her work and noted the high color in Liz's rigid face.

"Miriam, you have to tell them where you went after we had lunch."

"No. In this country, I don't," Miriam then smiled, "and I have the right to an attorney. Sit, Liz."

Liz began pacing.

Ach, always the pacing. "Come now, *Liebling*, calm down."

Liz stopped. She parked herself in the chair before Miriam's desk, and tears welled up in her eyes. "Please, I can't stand that they think you killed Addy. They might arrest you."

"Oh, I will tell them where I was—eventually, but right now, it must be kept quiet. Everything will be in place by the end of this week."

Liz pleaded, "Then, you'll tell them?"

Miriam grinned and shrugged her shoulders. "If they come back and ask next week, I'll tell them."

"What will you do if they take you in for questioning before then?"

"They have no grounds, Liz. They're fishing. They're not the Gestapo; only people trying to do their jobs. Besides, a woman who has watched her mother die taking a bullet for her can withstand anything." A sly smile crept onto her face, and she lifted her chin. "And what do you think my Gerald would do if they tried to take me away?"

Liz relaxed and laughed.

"No," Miriam continued, "it's you they will push and push. The truth will come out. And it won't take thirty-seven years like it did for me. You must stand firm."

"I will."

"And we will help. Now, there's work to be done."

Liz began to rise from her chair.

"Wait."

She sat again.

"I have chosen the three interns, and one of them is your brother."

"He deserves it?"

"Oh, his is a rare talent. He has a freshness, an innocence. And what is so wonderful, too, is that he's not spoiled. He is confident, but modest. I hope his internship here will inspire loyalty to our publishing house."

"Always thinking ahead, Miriam."

"Yes, it's good business. And, Liz, I'm assigning him to you."

Liz's jaw dropped and her eyes widened. "What? But . . . but . . ."

"I know. You have never had to put up with an intern."

"It's not that. It's just that—"

"He's your brother."

"And he doesn't know he's my brother. Miriam, I can't do this. Please assign him to someone else."

"It will be fine."

"No! It won't!" She looked like she was about to cross her arms and huff like a child having a tantrum.

"You are the only one other than myself to whom I would entrust such a talent. With you, he'll learn to appreciate what we publishers do for writers." Miriam smiled. "And—he'll get to know what a jewel you are."

"That won't matter because he'll never know about our connection. My father wanted to protect his family from the past? Then so be it."

"Your father is dead. His children are old enough to no longer need protection, and the dead are forgiven much."

Liz sprang up. "I don't care!" She began pacing.

Oy, the pacing again. "Liz, you are making me dizzy with this pacing."

She stopped. "Sorry. It's just—I don't want them scrutinizing me like some specimen from an inferior species. I had enough of that from Addy's mother, and I'll never put up with that kind of treatment again."

Miriam spoke calmly, "*Liebling*, only a stupid woman like Eunice Payne would think you inferior. From what I've seen of your brother, I don't believe your father's wife could be like her."

Liz stopped pacing and glared at Miriam. That expression was the same one Miriam remembered on Liz's face after she met with her father when she was nineteen; and it was clear the pain of his rejection had not faded over time.

"Of course," Miriam continued, "it's your life. But please get to know him. One day, you may be his link to this publishing house."

Liz trembled. "I'll mentor him—for you. But he must never know who I am. I don't want to go through. . . . I've had enough, Miriam."

Miriam softened at the pain in her eyes and nodded. Liz slipped out the door.

She stared at the door long after it had closed, bemused. Now, who is it that is in need of protection? She shook her head. Ah, my dear Liz, there are no accidents, but often second chances. Who should know better than I?

ᦞᦂTWELVEᦞᦂ

LIZ STROLLED ONTO her terrace. God, how she'd missed her home! The freshening evening breeze caressed her face and tickled her nose with the scent of roasting meats from some backyard grill in the neighborhood. It reminded her she hadn't eaten since lunch. City lights glowed and glimmered, jewels that hid the dowdier, ancient parts of Pittsburgh. She strolled toward the terrace parapet and looked down. Low floodlights barely illuminated the path. Despite how her mother died, heights never bothered her—dentists, yes, but not heights.

I love my nest, my aerie, where no one can reach me. She sighted the building housing Kernan, Feinstein and Company. I'm so blessed to be working at something I love in an industry where I'm respected. She glanced back at her living room and smiled. The perks aren't bad, either. However, what she treasured most were the people she loved—Miriam, Gerald, their children, and her good friends like Marisol.

A few years after her dream of becoming a part of her father's family turned into a sour memory, there was Addy—and their baby. She'd been so elated when she became pregnant. And although Addy grew distant and busier, she believed he would share her joy as soon as he saw his child. But she miscarried—and Addy's lack of compassion and his escalating drinking flagged the end of their marriage. She shrugged as if to shake off the past. This life I have now is enough . . . I am loved. That's more than enough. Let the past stay in the past. Wasn't happiness wanting what you already had?

Life without Addy and his demands was liberating, and yet guilt plagued her. Did he kill himself because I refused to loan him the money?

The passing clouds unveiled the moon, and its light glittered off something in the foliage far down the hill at the tall fence that enclosed the property from the drop-off. What is that? Trash? Liz shrugged her shoulders. Aluminum foil?

Diamonds glittered like that, although the object was too big to be a diamond. Glittering diamonds. Eunice Payne often wore them. How was Eunice dealing with Addy's death? The woman had ignored her calls and greeting cards since the divorce. It didn't make sense to force the issue, so Liz stopped trying to keep up a relationship with her.

She was glad she wasn't the one who had to tell her Addy was dead. Eunice had early on blinded herself to his short-comings and saw only the great ad man, Addison Tiffin Payne. The whole time she and Addy were married, if there wasn't an opportunity, Eunice would manufacture countless ones to show Liz that Addy deserved better than an illegiti-mate Polish girl. She had even callously faulted Liz for the miscarriage. And Addy's drinking? Eunice excused it—entertaining was part of his job. Of course, in the beginning, Liz had thought the same thing.

She crossed her arms, then retreated to one of the lounge chairs and sat. Well, I'm done with all of that now. If I'd given Addy the money, he would have just pissed it away.

He'd been heading down this dead-end road for some time. He could have chosen to get help instead of slowly kill-ing himself with booze. In any case, she had allowed guilt to have its way with her for far too long. It was time to march it out of her life.

But now there was a new problem. How am I going to deal with mentoring my brother? Liz realized that if she had insisted he be mentored by someone else, Miriam would have honored her wishes. Except, how do you say "no" to the peo-ple who gave you a second chance at life?

A chill passed through Liz, then comforting warmth. Are they here again? She glimpsed a mist forming at the bench near the parapet. Slowly, it coalesced into the translucent form of her dead mother. The scent of vanilla enveloped Liz, and she knew her grandmother must be there, too. Some-times her grandmother didn't appear, and only exuded a vanilla scent. Neither ever spoke, except when she dreamed about them, but she could rarely remember what they said. Her mother smiled at her and nodded. She was glad they vis-ited her. She felt good that they could see what she had made of her life.

The first time she had seen the spirit of a dead per-son was shortly after her grandmother died. Liz woke in the middle of the night and screamed when she saw her grand-mother at the foot of her bed and smelled the scent of vanilla. When her mother burst into the room, Liz could barely get the words out about what she'd seen.

"Don't be afraid, Lizzie. It's only Grandma. She just wants you to know she loves you and will be there for you. I never see her, but sometimes I feel her around me," Rayna said.

About a year after her mother jumped from the window of their third-story attic apartment, she, too, put in an ap-pearance. Liz wondered how someone who committed suicide could come back, because according to the Catholic Church, suicides were damned. However, the Kernans' pastor explained that God would not condemn a soul to an eternity in Hell when she was not in her right mind. He reminded her that they had celebrated a funeral mass for her mother and buried her in the Catholic cemetery.

Although she told Miriam and Gerald about the visits, Liz never felt she could share this experience with Addy. In fact, her mother and grandmother rarely appeared when she and Addy were together. They did appear at her wedding, but they weren't smiling, and they came often when she lost the baby. Her father never visited, nor any soul that could have been her baby. And she never saw other spirits.

The phone rang. Her mother and the vanilla scent faded.

"Hello?"

"Ms. Michaels? Detective Shannon here."

Liz said nothing.

"Ms. Michaels?"

"Yes, Detective. Are you still working?"

"Just finishing up some details before going home."

Home. Is home an empty apartment? He hadn't been wearing a wedding ring. Still, someone could be waiting for him, keeping dinner warm. "What do you need?"

"Nothing at the moment. Just wanted to check that you were able to get into your place."

"Yes."

"Everything the way it should be?"

"Yes."

"Good." He was silent a moment, and she thought he'd hung up. "Well . . . have a good evening."

"You, too."

Her stomach growled as she hung up the phone. She climbed the three steps to the foyer and entered the kitchen. In short order, a broiled, marinated Delmonico steak, a green salad, some French bread with parsley butter and a glass of a more than decent burgundy graced her table. She always treated herself to a formal setting, including candles and linen—a far cry from the crumb-strewn Formica dinette table of her childhood. As she sliced into the savory steak, she allowed herself a brief moment to imagine sharing such a meal with someone special.

✒️THIRTEEN

EUNICE PAYNE, HER body rigid, nostrils pinched, stood at the entrance to Liz's office and glowered at her. A flustered Mandy cowered behind her. Fortunately, the glass in the still shivering door remained intact. Like mother, like son. Had no one taught them to knock?

"Hello, Eunice. Please. Come in." Liz rose and gestured to the chairs in front of her desk."

Eunice stepped into the room and pinned Liz with stern eyes.

"Please, make yourself comfortable."

Color flushed Eunice's neck and face, making her look like an overworked boiler ready to blow. She glanced back at Mandy and looked ready to leap at her. Mandy stepped back and looked at Liz as though only she could rescue her from imminent immolation.

"Thank you, Mandy. You can take the manuscripts on the work table to their respective editors."

Mandy retreated but left the door open. Liz moved toward Eunice. "Eunice, I'm truly sorry for your loss. I know Addy meant the world to you." She put her hand on Eunice's shoulder. "If there's anything I can do to help, please let me know."

Eunice threw off Liz's hand and grasped the back of one of the chairs. Her breath came in short, growling gasps. "You. Murdering. Lying. Piece of trash!"

Liz recoiled but said nothing. This was grief. She knew it well.

"Why did you do it? Was it for the insurance?" Her eyes darted around the office. "Don't you have enough? I saw his place. How he was living. Nothing worth saving. You drained him of everything he had in the divorce! Did you have to take his life, too?" Eunice shook her head, tears splashing from her eyes, and crumpled into a chair.

Liz frowned, turned, and sat behind her desk again. She remained silent. Soon, Eunice stopped gasping, and her high color paled.

"I had no reason to harm Addy. I doubt there's an insurance policy, certainly not one with me as beneficiary. I don't think he could have afforded the premiums—and not because of any divorce settlement."

"But you could afford a policy on him!"

"Yes, I could afford a policy, but I don't need money."

Eunice's eyes wandered the office, and then finally hardened on Liz. "You were jealous of him! You couldn't stand it— couldn't stand how brilliant, how talented he was. You're just some nervy Polish slut who got lucky. No amount of money can change what you are. My Addy came of fine stock. Our heritage goes back to Ohio's earliest years."

Weary, Liz nodded. "Yes, yes, I know. You count Governor Edward Tiffin among your ancestors."

"Are you mocking me? How dare you!"

"No matter where we spring from, Eunice, we all have to face life's challenges as best we can—hopefully with grace."

Eunice humphed, and after a moment, glanced at Liz as though something had just occurred to her. "Why was Addy at your apartment?"

Liz shook her head. "I have no idea. I was here at work. He had no key, and the concierge would never have let him in."

"Suicide!" Eunice leaped from her seat, rose to her full height, and pointed at Liz. "You drove him to it, and he wanted you—wanted everyone—to know. That's what happened."

Liz thought of the money she refused to lend him. "The coroner hasn't ruled on cause of death, yet."

Eunice shook her head, "Yes, you killed him. You took my beautiful boy from me." The woman withered and shrank into herself.

Adelaide Hauser, who had been hovering outside the door to Liz's office, swept into the room and caught Eunice before she slumped to the floor.

"Mrs. Payne, it's time we go now." Adelaide stared coldly at Liz. "Come, we have a long drive, but there is tea and those little cakes you like in the car."

Eunice, looking more like a doddering woman in her nineties than the sixty-five she was, allowed her housekeeper to lead her from the office. She kept muttering, "My beautiful boy. My poor Addy," all the way through the outer office with Adelaide nodding and mumbling her agreement.

Liz got up and gently closed the door. She then returned to her desk and sat there with her face in her hands. She was weary of grief. Weary of guilt.

§⁊⊱⧽

"Shannon." He hugged the phone between jaw and shoulder while he continued to review the file before him. He welcomed the interruption. Wading through accumulated paperwork wore him down faster than an interrogation going nowhere. Santello should have been there, but Squires wanted them in the morgue. The paperwork threatened to bury both their desks, so they agreed one of them should pull desk duty while the other went to the morgue. He'd had enough of dead bodies, so Santello said she'd go and call if she thought he needed to see anything.

"Detective, this is Adelaide Hauser."

He retrieved the receiver from beneath his jaw. "Yes, Miss Hauser, what can I do for you?"

"Mrs. Payne would like to come in and talk to you."

Shannon could hear traffic noise in the background. "When?"

"I'm at a phone booth not far from the station. I'm sure we could be there in fifteen minutes or so."

He shook his head at the files on his desk and sighed. "I'll be here."

Shannon lost track of time. Head bowed over the file before him, he failed to see Eunice Payne at the side of his desk until the clerk cleared her throat.

He looked up and stood when he saw the woman. The clerk left, and he pointed to the chair beside his desk. "Mrs. Payne. Please. Have a seat."

The other detectives glanced at the dignified, diminutive woman in the navy Chanel suit and then continued with their own paperwork and interviews. The rumble of chatter, ringing phones, and typing came and went, underscored by the muffled sound of traffic outside the grimy windows. The air conditioning occasionally displaced the muggy air with ghosts of cool air, and the aroma of old coffee and abandoned lunches wafted through the large room like the bad memory of unsolved cases.

She situated herself on the hard wooden chair.

Shannon straightened his tie. "I can't vouch for the coffee, but would you like a cup—or perhaps tea or some water?"

"That won't be necessary, Detective." She appeared calm, sad, and tired. "I have some information that may help you with my son's case."

Tired or not, she still spoke with that low, velvety tone and caressed every word. Shannon sat and pulled his notebook out of his jacket. "What is it, Mrs. Payne?"

The small woman's eyes glittered like hard, cold diamonds. "It's about Liz Migielski."

"Who?"

She smiled like a Siamese cat. "Oh, that was her name before she changed it to Liz Michaels."

He sat back in his chair and waited.

She adjusted herself in the chair, folded her hands over the navy Coach bag in her lap, and pursed her lips. "About a year before she left my Addy . . ." She stopped after saying her son's name, then recovered. "Well . . . they were expecting, and she lost the baby."

"Oh." Shannon frowned. For a moment, he flashed back to his own loss.

"She blamed Addy."

"Why was that?"

"My son was busy with his career. She expected him to be there every moment, holding her hand—even after she lost the baby." She looked down at her hands. "We all mourned the loss, but life goes on." She raised her eyes and looked beyond Shannon's right shoulder. "That's why she left him."

"And you think this has something to do with your son's death?"

Eunice glared at him. "Don't be obtuse, Detective. She took everything Addy had, not to mention the outrageous alimony he told me he had to pay her."

Shannon wrote "alimony" in his notebook.

"Why, all he had was his work, his Jaguar, and his wardrobe. Appearances are very important in advertising, you know."

Shannon nodded.

"The last time I told him I was coming to visit for a few days, he said he'd moved into a small one-bedroom apartment temporarily because he was having work done on the house. So, of course, I stayed at a hotel." She shrank into herself. "Yesterday, we drove to the house to stop the work until I could decide what to do with the property. That's when we learned he'd sold it over a year ago." She stiffened and looked at Shannon as though he were responsible for Payne's lie. "We saw his apartment for the first time this morning. It was horrible! I wish he had come to me for help. He deserved better."

"Mrs. Payne, I'm truly sorry for your loss, but I don't understand what this has to do with your son's death."

Her hands flew to the arms of the chair, and she looked like she was about to launch herself at Shannon. "Revenge! Revenge and greed! I know that woman has a life insurance policy on him." She jabbed her finger at him. "You find that policy! She wanted revenge—revenge and the money from my son's death." Eunice burst into tears.

Shannon added the words "life insurance" with a question mark in his notebook.

The phone rang. It was Santello "Shannon, I want you to come down here and see what Squires found. He's still got Payne open."

He glanced at the woman weeping beside his desk. "Why?"

"You have to see this and hear what Squires thinks yourself. He can explain it better than I can. You're not going to believe your eyes."

"Okay, I'll be there as soon as I can."

He turned to Eunice. "Is Miss Hauser waiting for you up front?" She nodded. Shannon slipped into his jacket and escorted her out of the office.

६**FOURTEEN**ঌ

SHANNON'S EYES WIDENED when he saw the tattered aortic artery in Payne's chest cavity. "God, Squires, what is that?"

A big grin blossomed on the long, pock-scarred face of the tall, thin coroner. Shannon thought he looked like his name, like some old British actor playing a squire in an early forties movie. Of course, Squires was pure Pittsburgh. "Worst case I've ever seen. Thoracic aortic aneurysm."

"What the hell is that?"

"It's when part of the artery wall weakens and bulges out. Eventually the bulge grows thinner, and the artery finally bursts."

Santello added, "That's what killed Mona, too, not the cancer."

Shannon nodded.

Squires poked at the damaged tissue. "A rupture this bad is fast. A small percentage of people can survive if the vascular system is in better shape than Payne's, and they get help really fast. But most people don't make it. His would have been beyond repair." He shook his head. "He was dead before he hit the ground. The injuries from the fall support that, too. If he'd been conscious, he would have tensed his muscles, and we'd see a different pattern of damage."

"So, we don't have a homicide," Shannon said.

"So wrong, Seamus Aloysius," Santello said.

Shannon looked at her like she was missing the point, but Squires intervened. "Continuous, heavy consumption of alcohol eventually does a number on the organs, brain, and vascular system. He reeked, so I did the preliminary blood work right away. Alcohol level was high enough to poison a social drinker, but not him because his system was used to it."

Shannon threw up his hands. "Santello, it's still the aneurysm that killed him. It's not a homicide, so we can close the case."

She crossed her arms and shook her head. "Tell him, Doc."

Squires paused for effect. "What got this guy was enough amphetamine to power Duquesne Electric. Payne had a lousy cardiovascular system, but the combination of the drug with the alcohol likely triggered the burst artery."

"Likely?"

"Forget 'likely.' That artery should have done him in a long time ago, Shannon." Squires leaned against a stainless steel counter, holding his gloved hands in front of him. "No one—not even a drunk—would consume that much of the drug at one time. There were no pills in his stomach. Someone dissolved a huge amount of amphetamine in the liquor he drank."

Santello glowered at Shannon. "Think it's time for the murder book?"

Shannon glanced at the mess in Payne's open body and nodded. A vision of blue eyes that could turn from a tranquil lagoon to a raging arctic storm claimed his mind. I hope it's not her.

ᏚᎡFIFTEENᏚᎡ

EUNICE SLAMMED THE receiver down. She'd caught the editor at the *Pittsburgh Post Gazette* before he left for home. He talked to her as though he were speaking to a child when he explained that he could not print what she told him about Liz Michaels, only those facts that had been provided by the police. Such excuses would not have been tolerated in her father's time when news people took the words of their betters as gospel. But now, everyone was so afraid of lawsuits. "Humph."

She tapped the desk with manicured nails and pondered her options. Suddenly, her eyes sparkled. *The Triangle Tattler*. She had never read the rag, but it was apparently a popular Pittsburgh version of those national gossip tabloids, and the nephew of one of her acquaintances was a reporter for that publication. This woman desperately wanted to join the country club but needed a sponsor. Eunice had detoured around the issue because the woman's wealth came from an ex-husband involved in a lucrative but questionable import-export business. Money, after all, did not make everyone acceptable; however, this was for Addy. Wealth alone would now have to suffice as a basis for Eunice's sponsorship—provided the woman was cooperative, of course. She found her number in her thick address book, dialed, and brokered a deal.

Eunice looked at her watch. Now was a good time to contact the governor's wife. Those politicos had cronies all over the country, and the governor's wife was from a well-connected Pittsburgh family. After hearing Eunice's version of Addy's death and Liz's involvement, the governor's wife agreed to contact the wife of the Pittsburgh District Attorney as well as the wife of the Mayor. She was well acquainted with both women and would encourage them to use their influence to bring pressure on the investigation. That done, Eunice then began her marathon calls to the considerable number of gossips in her address book. Her dried lips formed a smile. Word of mouth was often more effective than the media.

ᢏᢢ᠅SIXTEEN᠅ᢢᢏ

SHANNON APPROACHED LIZ Michaels' apartment. She'd agreed to meet him at her home when he called her late that afternoon. Santello grumbled about missing the interview because she had to take her mother and grandmother to their weekly bingo fix. However, she demanded to check the divorce settlement and search for any life policies on Payne the following day. Shannon had no objection to Santello's absence or her desire to take on the research. He looked forward to seeing Liz Michaels alone.

Santello's check on cab companies for the day Payne died produced nothing except the record from Liz's regular cab provider. It logged her ride to work in the morning and her return home around five thirty. Santello insisted Michaels could easily have taken a bus and then the Incline up Mt. Washington to her apartment that afternoon. "Then she could have poisoned her ex, pushed him off the terrace, and made it back to the office in time to leave work at five thirty. "After all," she quipped, "who else could have let him into her place?"

Santello confirmed that their earlier background check on Michaels revealed she'd changed her name after graduating from Pitt. "Didn't you read the report?"

He'd grinned like a three year old who'd jumped into a big mud puddle after being told not to. "Uh, I glanced at it."

Santello shook her head and scowled. "Seamus Aloysius, one of these days, you're going to miss something very important."

He rang the doorbell and his stomach rumbled. Tonight would be another late dinner. Shannon couldn't abide the flavorless, high-calorie treats in the machines at the station, and fast food gave him gas. He knew his sister would have saved him something for dinner. It was worth waiting for good food.

When Liz opened the door, the aroma of roast beef made his mouth water. It smelled every bit as good as Eileen's. He again registered her astonishing blue eyes. The rest of her face was subdued. It wasn't hard to understand why after their last interview at her office. Beige linen shirt and slacks complemented her icy blond looks. It had been another humid day, and Shannon felt rumpled in his gray suit. He wondered if his deodorant was still working and hoped the cooking scents would cover any failure.

"Come in, Detective."

He hesitated. "Am I interrupting your dinner?"

"No, I've just finished."

She led him to the living room and sat in one of the armchairs. Shannon sat on the sofa and again noted the unusual painting above the fireplace. Although different in style, color, and setting, it reminded him of the Cassatt print in her office. He wondered what she liked about this painting. Maybe it has something to do with her lost child. Contrary to what Santello thought, he did pay attention to details.

"That picture," he indicated with a nod of his head, "reminds me of the Cassatt print in your office."

She almost smiled and nodded her head. "*The Boating Party.* I have copies of some of her other paintings, too. This painting is by my friend Marisol Sanchez. She gave it to me when—" Pain flickered in her eyes and then was gone. "It was a gift. . . . Have you heard of Marisol?"

So the painting did have something to do with the baby. "No, I haven't, but I'm not up on the latest in art. I do know something about Cassatt, though. Did you know she was from around here?"

"Yes, I knew that." Liz sat back and regarded him. "I'm surprised. Few men are interested in her work."

"My wife—my late wife—was into the Impressionists."

A look of concern crossed her features. "Oh." She looked like she was about to express her condolences but didn't. "So, why did you want to see me?"

"Eunice Payne visited me this afternoon."

Liz grimaced. "That's interesting. She visited me right before lunch."

"Hm. She didn't mention that to me."

"Yes, she's convinced I'm responsible for Addy's death. I'm surprised she didn't claw my eyes out or have a stroke." Liz glanced at Marisol's painting and her face softened. "I know Addy was her only son, but I don't appreciate being the target of her rage."

Shannon shifted forward on the sofa and pulled out his notebook. He knew what was in it and didn't expect to add more to it, but the notebook helped him distance himself from her. "Her visit raised some questions."

"Yes, I'm sure it did."

Shannon lowered his eyes to his notebook. "She seems to think . . . that your behavior in the divorce was motivated by revenge . . . and that everything you walked away with wasn't enough." Then he glanced up and fixed his eyes on her, a maneuver that usually made suspects squirm.

She returned his stare. "What did I walk away with? I only took my clothes and Marisol's painting. I wanted no reminders of my life with Addy; I just wanted out."

"What about the alimony?"

Liz laughed and gestured at her surroundings. "Detective, you see my home. I'm part owner of Kernan, Feinstein and Company. What judge would grant me alimony, especially from an unemployed man whose bank account was rapidly approaching zero? This is Pittsburgh, not LA."

He nodded, no expression on his face. "Did you have a life insurance policy on him?"

Liz rolled her eyes. "Oh, that. One of the stipulations of the settlement was that we each could carry life insurance on the other. And, no, I never took out a policy on Addy. I wanted nothing more to do with him."

"Whose idea was it to make that part of the settlement?"

She shrugged her shoulders. "I'm not sure. It may have been Addy's lawyer—maybe the judge. I wanted the divorce done and over with, so I didn't care, and my lawyer saw no problem with it. He said either of us could probably take out a policy on the other without it being stipulated in the settlement anyway."

Shannon put away his notebook and stood to go. She walked him to the door. With his hand on the doorknob, he turned to her. "Ms. Michaels, do you use alcohol or diet pills?"

Liz cocked her head to the side. "Why would you ask me that?"

"Well, do you?"

She stood taller and lifted her head. "I usually have a glass of wine with dinner, but I'm not a drinker, don't keep liquor around—not even beer. And I'm no junkie. I need to be focused for my work. I have too much responsibility to risk getting squirrely on diet pills. And, anyway, I've never had a weight problem."

"Uh-huh." Shannon opened the door and said, "Well, thank you for meeting with me so late."

"Yes, it is late. I hope you've had your dinner."

Shannon nodded and wished her a good night. As she closed the door, he caught a last glimpse of her eyes—now a little warmer—and drifted to the elevator.

Was she going to ask me if I wanted something to eat? I hope Eileen fixed something as good as what I smelled in there. He pressed the down button. No way could this woman have killed Payne.

ξつてつ3

Liz leaned against the closed door and spotted the spirits of her mother and grandmother in the living room. They smiled at her. "Was I really going to offer him dinner? Just because his wife is dead, doesn't mean he lives on TV dinners . . . a man like him—there's probably a girlfriend. Besides, I don't think he'd eat dinner prepared by a suspect."

As usual, her mother and grandmother remained silent. They vanished, their smiles and the vague scent of vanilla the last vestiges of their presence.

§⁊⁊⁊⁊⁊

The man lying next to her hugged her close. She heard him inhale her scent. Then she felt his lips like butterflies on her shoulder and his hand glide down her body. She turned to face her lover and gazed into the gentle eyes of Jim Shannon. This was so right. He was the—

Liz awoke to the annoying buzz of her alarm clock, arching her back, aware of sensations she hadn't felt in some time. "Hooh," she said, "must have been quite a dream." But she couldn't remember very much of it. Who was the man? She supposed it was only natural she had a dream like that. It had been some time since she'd shared her bed with anyone.

She'd tried the friend with benefits route, but it was too much like skim milk when what she really wanted was a rich, creamy chocolate milkshake. Maybe, if she was lucky, that compassionate, loyal, lovable man would come along some day. With a hint of a smile, she shook her head at her hopeful heart and headed to the bathroom for her shower.

⟡ SEVENTEEN ⟡

SANTELLO LOOKED UP from her paperwork. "You're late. . . . Long night?" She continued looking at him with arched eyebrows and the shadow of a smirk.

Shannon yawned as he plopped into his chair. "Overslept. Didn't hear the alarm, and Eileen thought I'd already left."

Santello tapped her pen on the desk. "Captain McIlheny says since Squires declared Payne's death a homicide, the DA wants a suspect in custody pronto. We're needed on other cases."

"Yeah? Well, I'd like a cool, breezy day right now instead of this heat and humidity. Ain't gonna happen."

"Money's tight, Shannon. Like June, the budget's bustin' out all over."

"Just because the DA wants someone in custody doesn't mean we have enough to arrest anyone." He paused and squinted at her. "Where's McIlheny?"

"Why?"

"Because I have a feeling that a certain wealthy, grieving mother has the ear of our esteemed DA, and McIlheny will know if that's what's at the bottom of this push for an arrest."

"So what, Shannon. Look, someone had to let Payne into the Ice Queen's palace. The crime scene investigators didn't find any keys or lock picks on him. No liquor bottle either, not even a flask on him. She did it and took the liquor and amphetamine with her."

Shannon sighed and shook his head. "The Kernans have a key, and so does the concierge. A lot of people like this woman. Maybe someone likes her enough to make her life less complicated. I want to check them all out. I didn't like the way Mrs. Kernan refused to tell you where she went after her lunch with Michaels. And her husband was supposedly out of town that day. We should run that down. How about Michaels' assistant? Think she might have a key Michaels forgot about?"

Santello shrugged and raised her eyebrows. "So, a lot of people like Michaels, and maybe one of those people liked her enough to murder her ex? That's filling the suspect pool with a lot of red herrings, Seamus Aloysius." She picked up a pencil and squinted at the print along the side. "You like her, too—so much so, you're trying to pin this on someone other than the most likely suspect."

He put his arms on the desk, leaned across it, and looked her in the eyes. "It's called investigating, Santello. And my gut tells me she didn't kill him."

"Well, my gut doesn't agree with your gut."

Shannon scowled. "Why are you so sure she's guilty? Is it because she looks so much like Mona, and you can't stand that she's alive and Mona's gone?"

Santello stiffened. "It's got nothing to do with my Mona. Mona's dead and that's the end of it."

Shannon couldn't stop himself. "And nobody can take her place. Is that it?"

Santello's face flushed. "If you want to play shrink, take a look at yourself, Shannon."

Shannon's face colored, and his eyes glistened with tears. The room got very quiet. The other detectives studied their desks as though they had just discovered them.

She caught the look on his face. "Sorry, Shannon. Guess we both got a little out of bounds. . . . But maybe you don't want it to be her because you like her." Her eyes softened. "I can understand that."

Shannon cleared his throat and rose abruptly. "I'm just tired. Want some coffee?"

Santello shook her head. The room gradually returned to its normal dull buzz.

When Shannon entered the tiny, crowded room they used for storage and as a break room, he found McIlheny pouring himself a cup of the brown liquid that passed for coffee. "Cap."

"Shannon. . . . So, how's the case coming? Making any progress?"

"Yeah, look, about that." Shannon fixed two coffees, and McIlheny waited, blowing on his own mug. "I understand our caseload is bigger than it's ever been, and money's tight, but we just don't have enough to arrest anybody."

"The DA wants what you have so far. Thinks he can make a case."

"He thinks he can make a case, or someone is pressuring him?" Shannon refused to release the older man from his stare.

McIlheny didn't turn away, didn't blink. Finally he took a sip of his coffee and turned to leave. "Just get the job done, Shannon."

Shannon shook his head as McIlheny disappeared into his office. He then snatched the mugs off the counter and returned to his desk. He placed one of the coffees on Santello's desk, stretched out in his chair, and grinned at her.

She glanced at the mug and then up at him. "Did I ask for this?"

He gulped a good mouthful from his mug. "You'll want it in an hour or so. Isn't that how you like your coffee? Iced?"

Santello chuckled. "Okay, Shannon."

"Talked to McIlheny."

"Yeah?"

"I asked him about the DA. He didn't come out and say there was pressure, but I got the feeling from the way he acted that there was."

Santello sighed and shook her head. "So what do we do next?"

"Well . . . let's check out Payne's apartment and find out where he got his liquor. There must be some bars nearby or a liquor store. We can run down the other possibilities later."

"Good. By the time we get back, my coffee should be just right."

Mr. Campbell, the tall, snowy-haired building superintendent, unlocked Payne's door and answered Santello's question. "No, never saw him bring anyone here or get any visitors. Course, I don't sit around spying on all the tenants, so he could have had company when I wasn't around." He shook his head. "He wasn't like some of them with people coming round making noise all times of the day and night."

"Mr. Payne's mother came by yesterday morning, didn't she?" Shannon asked.

Campbell raised his sharp blue eyes. "Yeah, her and her friend. Came to get his stuff. They didn't take much. Said I could do what I wanted with the furniture. Acted like it all smelled bad. Paid me a few bucks to help carry stuff to her car."

"What did they take?" Santello said.

"His clothes, a real nice suitcase, a briefcase, and some files—oh—and a real pretty painting of horses with riders in them red jackets rich people wear when they go riding. He had it in his bedroom."

Campbell paused a moment and stroked his veined nose. "I was a little embarrassed for him, though. He left a trash can full of liquor bottles. Not a fit sight for a mother who's lost her son. I tried to stand in front of it so they wouldn't see it, but I had to move so I could help carry stuff to the car. Mrs. Payne looked at them bottles, then got all huffy and acted like they wasn't there."

Both Santello and Shannon nodded their heads. "Any idea where Payne did his drinking?" Shannon asked.

"Word around here, he made the rounds and ran up his tabs. There's a bar on about every block in this neighborhood." He scratched his chin. "But he did tell me his favorite place was Busch's in Southside. It's not far. Said any time I'd like to join him, he could get me free drinks. Told him I've been on the wagon for twenty-three years, and if I started drinking again, it'd kill me."

"Thanks, Mr. Campbell. We'll let you know when we're done here."

Campbell handed over the key. "Just lock up and drop the key in the box by my door. Gotta get some groceries and be back in time for *Wheel of Fortune*." He turned to leave. "Oh, haven't touched anything except throw out them bottles. Plenty of time to clean up and get rid of this stuff." He looked around and scratched his chin again. "Maybe I can rent it furnished for a few more bucks." He winked. "Landlord would love that."

They entered Payne's apartment and took in the cheap dark paneling, dusty brown drapes, and spotted, worn gold carpeting. Dust motes danced through shards of sunlight that squeeze past gaps in the drapes. Goodwill rejects littered the dim living area. A chrome and Formica dining table and two chairs, once popular in the fifties, were pushed against the bar separating the tiny kitchen from the rest of the place. It smelled of disinfectant, old dust, and spent hopes.

The detectives made their way to the bathroom, which was only big enough for a rusting shower stall, toilet, and small sink overhung by a medicine chest with a cracked mirror. Curling green linoleum and walls thick with several layers of muddy gold paint, swirled like shiny frosting, completed the decor. Shannon opened the medicine chest. It contained one lone bottle of aspirin.

Neither of them said anything, but they cocked their heads and looked at each other when they edged into the bedroom. Although the bed was unmade, the room looked to be in better shape. Payne had at least invested in a decent mattress, pillows, and linens.

Santello said it all: "Dead man walking."

EIGHTEEN

LIZ BREEZED BY Mandy's desk.

"Your intern is here," Mandy called after her.

Liz froze, darting her eyes around the room. "Where is he?" She spun around. "Not in my office?"

"No. I sent him to Personnel for orientation."

Liz let out her breath. "Good. . . . I'd forgotten the interns were starting today. I'm really not ready for him."

"What would you like me to do with him when he gets back?"

"Send him over to Reid so he can see how manuscripts are winnowed, and tell him I'm sorry I couldn't meet with him today, but we'll get together tomorrow."

"Okay, Liz."

Liz was about to enter her office when Mandy rushed up to her. "Oh, Liz, Mrs. Kernan left this for you. She said you should look it over as soon as possible."

The portfolio was labeled "Ivar Arnesson." Liz rolled her eyes and grabbed it. She turned into her office, closed the blinds on the windows separating her from the outer office, and plopped down in her chair. Elbows on the desk, she ran her fingers through her short hair and stared at the portfolio that contained her half-brother's information and writing. She sighed and flipped through the pages of information until she found the manuscript.

A couple of hours past quitting time, she finished the story, her face tear-damp. He had captured her with the first sentence and touched her to her very core with the story of a young boy struggling with the loss of his father. It was fiction, but she knew that it sprang from his own experience and from wisdom far beyond his years. It was not only well written, but showed her a side of their father she hadn't suspected—a tender, whimsical, caring man who would do anything for his family.

This depiction was so different from her own experience with him. Or was it? He'd had no idea who the young woman was who followed him into that downtown Pittsburgh café. She'd not considered the shock she gave him. All she knew was that she ached horribly over her mother's suicide. Her death was an abandonment, nothing like the natural passing of her grandmother. It marked an end, leaving Liz with the task of making a beginning that would fill the emptiness.

All those years her mother refused to tell her about her father, and what did she do? The night before she made her exit through that damned window, she finally shared everything about him, even why she would not marry him. He sympathized when she told him about Rayna, wanted to help her—with money, with a job at his insurance company where they could get to know each other. However, taking her into his family was not an option. Because he'd never revealed his relationship with Rayna and the existence of his illegitimate daughter to his wife, he feared his dishonesty would destroy their marriage and damage their family.

And the family? The wife in the story was nothing like the cold, selfish woman Liz believed her father's wife to be. She felt she could easily have become friends with this woman and the sisters portrayed in the story. Were they really like he depicted them? If they were, then why was her father so afraid of his wife's reaction? Maybe the boy manipulated the details to suit his story, even changing a cold woman into the proverbial earth mother.

Regardless of whatever the reality might be, Miriam knew what she was talking about: He was born to write. Many established writers didn't have this boy's skill. No doubt, his writing would become more sophisticated, his voice even stronger, over time. She tapped her pen on the manuscript. He very well could be his generation's iconic writer.

The young man inched into Liz's office with a mug of coffee, a napkin, and a plate containing a pastry and fork. He handed them to her and smiled. The space between his teeth was so much like her own. "Mandy asked me to bring these in to you, Ms. Michaels. By the way, I'm Paddy Arnesson."

Anxiety stiffened her body. She hoped she didn't come across as unfriendly. It wasn't his fault their father had rejected her. Liz nodded and gazed at the young man she'd nearly collided with outside of Miriam's office. Now she understood why he'd looked so familiar. Except for his coloring, they did look like they were related, especially since they shared the same space between their teeth.

"You're allowed to have coffee and pastry, too, you know. We're pretty informal around here."

"Yeah, Mandy offered me some, but I've had my coffee, and, honestly, I'm too nervous to eat."

"Have a seat." Liz forked a bit of the pastry into her dry mouth and tried to smile. "My only vice." She coughed and sipped her coffee before managing a second bite, which threatened to stick in her throat as well. She took another sip of coffee and abandoned the pastry. "So, what do you expect to get from this internship?"

He took a deep breath and leaned forward. "Two things. First, I want to understand how a publishing house works. Second," he grinned, "I hope that Kernan, Feinstein and Company will publish my work."

Her face relaxed into a soft smile. "The first, I can guarantee. The second, we'll see. We nurture talent here, but we don't have much tolerance for boorish writers no matter how good they are."

Paddy laughed. "I've met some of those boorish writers. A few of them were invited to talk to us in my writing classes. I think I know what you mean. Not pretty. I learned not to ask any questions after getting the you-dumb-little-idiot-you'll-never-be-as-good-as-I-am stare."

Liz warmed up to him. "Exactly, although they were probably thinking something far worse than 'idiot.'"

He grinned. "Uh-huh, that's the feeling I got, but I didn't want to say it."

"I read your manuscript."

Paddy blushed. "I'm still revising it. It's not finished."

"Nevertheless, it's quite promising. How did you come up with the idea?"

"I based the story on my father's death and how it affected all of us, but it is fiction."

"I see. And are all your characters like the people in your family?"

"Pretty much—no, that's not true. My family's nicer, but I didn't think my characters would be interesting without a few faults. And the boy in my story is the oldest—not the youngest like me, only has two sisters—I have three, and has no uncles or aunts. Also, my family is in better financial shape than the family in my story."

Nicer? Ivar Arnesson must not have felt that way. "You're very fortunate. This is a tough world. Without people in your life who care about you, you could end up pretty lost."

He nodded.

"Yesterday, you worked with the readers, right?"

"Yes, I couldn't believe how quickly they went through manuscripts. Harold—Mr. Reid—explained how they did it and had me try it later in the afternoon. I thought the readers were being mean when they rejected some of the manuscripts after only reading the first page, but then I realized if the beginning was bad, the rest of the manuscript probably wasn't worth reading, and I found that to be the case. It taught me the importance of having a great beginning if I want my manuscript to make it into the hands of an editor."

Liz laughed. "You'll have an agent to make sure your work is ready for a publisher's eyes. We still accept unrepresented submissions because sometimes we do find a gem." She sipped her coffee. "I'd like you to go back to the readers today. I'll get you later if something I think you should see pops up. Anyway, I'll stop by before the end of the day. Tomorrow, we'll plan a schedule of your rotation through the various departments of the company."

"Sure." He stood to go, then hesitated. "I hope you don't think I'm out of line here, but I notice we have something in common."

Startled, Liz looked up and waited.

"When you laughed, I noticed that you have a space between your teeth just like mine." Paddy smiled, blushing. "We could be from the same family."

Liz's eyes widened, then she pressed her lips together. "No, you're not out of line. It's normal to want to connect in some way with people, especially your mentor. I keep meaning to get it fixed, but I don't much like dentists. You have a problem with dentists, too?"

"No. My mother just doesn't see any reason to spend money on a cosmetic procedure. She'd rather give the money to a free clinic. Once I'm making money, I plan to get it fixed—and, to keep my mother happy, I'll send a contribution to a charity, too." He was thoughtful a moment. "Sometimes, though, I think it's because it reminds her of my father."

"But you don't really look like him."

"What?"

Liz fumbled with her coffee mug. "Well, Paddy, you look so Irish, and with a name like Arnesson, I assume your father was Swedish. I always thought most Swedes had very fine, straight blond hair—at least, the ones I know do. You don't look Swedish. Was your father blond?" He nodded and gave her an uncertain smile. As he turned to leave, she added, "Oh, by the way, you can call me 'Liz' since we're going to be working together."

"Okay . . . Liz."

Once he was gone, she melted into her chair and sighed. She was going to have to watch herself. Then again, how would he react if he discovered who she was? He might hate her for revealing a side of their father that would disappoint him. Would he tell his mother? Or would he keep it secret so she could keep the fond memories she had of her dead husband? He seemed like the kind of kid who would do that.

Of course, he might be thrilled to discover he was related to one of the owners of Kernan, Feinstein and Company, and if his mother was really as loving as the mother in his book, she might welcome the secret daughter of her late husband.

Liz pulled the pastry towards her and tore off a piece, then tossed it into the wastebasket. It was all so nerve-rackingly complicated. Her life was finally on an even keel, and she liked it that way. There had been too many storms. No, the least threatening course of action for everyone would be to remain the secret her father took to his grave.

༄༅

Miriam, arms crossed, leaned against Liz's door frame. "So?"

Liz glanced up from her work and leaned back in her chair. "You're right. He's a very talented writer."

"It must run in the family."

"What? Are there more writers in that family?"

"I don't know about that family. I'm talking about you. You, too, are a skilled writer."

Liz shook her head. "Perhaps, but I don't have the passion for it. I'd rather prepare and eat a gourmet dinner than write the not-so-great American novel. Besides, I'm much more interested in the business end of producing literature, and I'm good at it."

"That you are," said Miriam, sitting down.

"He's confident but not egotistical. Does he have an agent, yet? We should get him under contract."

"I'm glad your assessment agrees with mine. Discuss it with him."

"There's one thing, though."

Miriam cocked her head.

"If I continue to work closely with him, I'm afraid I'm going to let it slip that I'm his sister. I almost gave myself away, today." Liz told Miriam about her slip and how she'd explained it away.

Miriam laughed. "Did he believe you?"

"I hope so."

"Would it really be so terrible for him to learn that you are his sister? You read his book. It's probably reflective of his family."

"He said his family was nicer than the characters in his book."

"There. You see. If they knew about you, they would probably welcome you into their lives. I know you always believed that your father's wife was a cold woman, but perhaps you were seeing it all through your father's rejection, although he did want to give you a job at his insurance company so you could get to know each other." Miriam shook her head. "Sometimes, I wonder if we should have pushed you harder to meet with him again."

"You know the harder you pushed, the more I would have resisted."

Miriam nodded, remembering the young Liz. "Yes, you could be incredibly stubborn." She sat in one of the chairs across from Liz. "You know, maybe your father wanted to be sure you were the kind of person he would want his family to meet. I mean, for all practical purposes, you were a stranger to him. You could have been a con artist, even a murderer."

"Oh, Miriam, a murderer!"

Miriam shrugged. "Well, you must admit what a shock your sudden appearance and the news of your mother's death must have been."

"Yes, I understand that now, but I felt so lost then. I just wanted him to claim me, to be my father, to make me part of his family."

"A meeting with you and us together may have reassured him."

"He could have come after me when I ran off after our meeting, but he didn't."

"Perhaps he looked for you, but how would he have found you? Your mother's apartment was in her husband's name, and he was gone. Remember, that very afternoon, we moved you in with us, and your landlady had no interest in where you were moving."

Liz stared at her. "In all this time, I never considered that. I figured he didn't want me in his life because he was afraid he would lose his family. That is what he said."

"Oh perhaps. More likely, he was afraid of facing his wife's disappointment because he had kept something so important from her. From what you told me, he said that honesty between them was very important to her."

"Do you think she would have forgiven him?"

"She would have felt betrayed that he kept such a secret from her, but, yes, if she loved him as much as the mother in Paddy's book loved her husband, I think so . . . in time." She looked at her watch. "Let's get some lunch."

❧❦NINETEEN❧❦

LIZ AND MIRIAM gazed out the window from their favorite table in Vinaigrette. They enjoyed watching people scurry ahead of others while some traipsed along the busy sidewalks and stopped here and there to point at whatever caught their interest. What they relished most, however, was a white-gloved policeman who directed traffic in the manner of a renowned symphony conductor. He even sometimes performed a pirouette. So many people talked about the officer that a reporter had immortalized his routine on film, and KDKA had broadcast it on the eleven o'clock news. Now the traffic cop was a tourist attraction, and the local merchants and eateries experienced a modest increase in business.

Liz and Miriam came here often, not only for the entertainment, but because whatever Vinaigrette served was always fresh that day—often from the owner's country garden during the growing season.

The hostess led a group of four chattering women into the dining room. When they saw Liz, they lagged behind.

"That's her!" a silver-haired, well-dressed woman said to the others.

They eyed one another as though assaulted by the odor of sewage. Liz recognized all four of them from some of the parties Eunice dragged them to whenever she visited them in Pittsburgh.

"I can't believe she has the nerve to appear in public," a hefty, middle-aged redhead said. "Why hasn't she been arrested?"

The hostess, now at the far end of the room, turned around and pointed to a table only to discover her flock had not followed her. She waved to them. "Ladies, will this table do?"

The women mumbled among themselves and swept past Liz and Miriam as though they were invisible.

Miriam lifted her eyebrows. "Acquaintances of yours?"

"Eunice's friends." Liz rolled her eyes. "Looks like she's started her smear campaign. Well, I did say, one way or another, Eunice would make me pay for Addy's death."

Miriam looked down at her empty plate. "She's not relying entirely on word-of-mouth to punish you."

"What do you mean?"

"Jeff Darnley over at the *Post-Gazette* called me this morning. He told me Addy's mother called him the other day to get him to publish an article on Addy's death that was—let's see, how did he put it—'heavy with her opinion about your involvement.' Of course, he told her that they could only publish facts and were under some constraint by the authorities since this was an ongoing investigation. Jeff suggested she talk to the police about her suspicions. He's kept a very cool hand on the reporting of this incident. He knows you're incapable of harming another human being. However, he did advise me to read this week's *Triangle Tattler*."

"Don't tell me."

Miriam pulled the folded tabloid from her large purse and placed it on the table.

Liz looked down and read. When she reached the end, she shook her head, her face flushed with anger.

"It's borderline, but I don't think they've wandered into lawsuit territory. I'll have our attorney check it out."

"Don't bother." Liz folded and placed the paper on her plate. "Who reads this rag anyway? Besides, not responding will assure it a quick death." The olive oil on her plate crept into the paper, and Liz was tempted to add more, however, fine olive oil deserved better. She sighed and slumped back in her chair. "As angry as this makes me and as much as I dislike Eunice, I keep telling myself she's doing this because she's lost her only child."

Miriam was quiet a moment. "We all lose loved ones. She, however, won't quit until she has ruined you—or worse. Be careful, Liz. Vengeful people can be unpredictable and dangerous. Perhaps it's time for a long vacation? Go visit Marisol in Santa Fe."

"I don't think those detectives would let me—at least, not until this is settled."

"Then I think it would be best if you stayed with us for the time being."

Liz smiled and shook her head. "I'll be fine, Miriam. Really. My gosh, she's sixty-five, you know."

"You are so stubborn," Miriam said and drained the last of her coffee.

Liz grinned and pulled out her credit card to pay the bill. It was her turn today. "Gerald said we'd be meeting with Abe sometime this week to finalize the sale."

Miriam rested her bag on her lap and was silent a moment. "It might not be this week."

"Why?"

"His wife apparently heard your ex-mother-in-law's version of Addy's death from the mayor's wife and saw a copy of that rag, and now Abe fears a scandal involving you would cast a shadow over the reputation of his company. He wants to wait until this blows over. Gerald didn't want to say anything to you about it right away since he believed you would be quickly cleared of any involvement."

Liz shook her head. "But Abe knows me."

"Oh, I'm sure he doesn't doubt your innocence." Miriam waved her hand. "We can wait. We have a six-month exclusive agreement with him."

"I don't suppose it would help if I talked to Abe myself?"

Miriam shrugged. "What do you think?"

Liz looked down at the vestiges of her lunch and shook her head. Abe Perkins was somewhat of a local blue blood, his family going back to the early settlement of Pittsburgh. He took as much pride in William Penn Press as he did in his ancestry.

The waiter returned with Liz's credit card and receipt, but she didn't put them away. The restaurant with its aromas and clatter of cutlery faded. Images of all her times with the Kernans upstaged the present—all they had done for her, how they had cared for her, how they had loved her. She grabbed the card and receipt and stuffed them in her purse, then waited until Miriam looked at her.

"I want to relinquish my ownership in the company and re-sign my position."

Miriam raised her eyes to the ceiling and shook her head. "Gerald said you would suggest something like this."

"It's not a suggestion."

"*Liebling*, the people we love are more important to us than the purchase of another publishing company."

"But—"

"More important than this company. More important than money, of which we already have plenty."

"But—"

"No. You have more than earned your interest in Kernan, Feinstein and Company. You are its heart and soul."

Liz opened her mouth, but at Miriam's stern look, closed it. This was one argument she would never win. She smiled and held back her tears. She really would have hated giving up the company.

ϾϟϟTWENTYϟϟϿ

ARRANGED SQUARELY ON her late husband's desk, an insurance policy on Liz Michael's life for five hundred thousand dollars and her son's flow chart absorbed Eunice Payne's complete attention. She discovered the documents hidden in the false bottom of Addy's briefcase, which was the same as his father's—actually a gift from the old man. After her husband's heart attack and death, she'd found several hundred thousand dollars in bearer bonds in the false bottom of his own briefcase.

Because Addy was obviously strapped for money, she puzzled over why he would buy such an expensive policy—until she looked closely at the flow chart titled "Ad Agency Startup." Under the box labeled "Financing" were four boxes listing possible sources—"The Bank," "Investors," "Mother" and "Liz." The first three were crossed out with red marker. Eunice sobbed at seeing herself crossed off. She would gladly have helped him make his dream a reality. She could have provided him with investors as well. Beneath Liz's name, two boxes contained the words "If Yes—Full Speed Ahead" and "If No." Beneath the "If No" box were two more boxes. One contained the words "Reconcile with Liz" and the other "Insurance Policy." All of the boxes except for "Insurance Policy" were almost completely filled in with red slashes. The "Insurance Policy" box was circled in green marker, and he'd used that marker to write "Go for it!" beneath it.

Eunice now understood why he was in Liz's apartment, and she was not shocked at what he intended to do. She leaned back in her chair. That white trash owed him, and he was going to collect. Tears leaked from her bloodshot eyes. But that *thing* took his precious life instead. Eunice dabbed her face. Damn her! I know she was there! Addy's dead because of her, and now I'm going to make her pay.

She'd learned her word-of-mouth smear campaign and the tabloid article had little effect on Liz's career. And the pressure the DA brought to bear on the police did not lead to a speedy arrest. Eunice opened the side drawer, which contained the gun chest housing her late husband's revolver. She lifted the lid and inhaled the scent of oil and metal. She removed the weapon from the chest and caressed it.

Oh, my sweet boy, I'll really make her pay! Addy was the third major loss of her life, not including her husband and parents. Their deaths were no loss to her. But the other two losses had nearly unhinged her. Now that Addy was gone, she had nothing to live for but vengeance. She kissed the weapon and placed it back into its cushioned bed. She had a funeral to arrange first.

 formula

Later that night, Adelaide Hauser made her routine inspection of the mansion. In the den, she stared at the policy and flow chart, frozen as if Medusa had turned her to stone. She understood what she was seeing. Should she inform the police about this discovery or should she remain loyal to Mrs. Payne? It would be such a scandal if her son's intentions became public.

The gun!

Adelaide opened the deep side drawer of the desk and saw the chest that contained the gun. She opened the chest, relieved to find the gun still there. As much as Mrs. Payne hated the Michaels woman, she had too much class to shoot her former daughter-in-law. Adelaide almost laughed out loud as she pictured Mrs. Payne wielding a gun. She could swing a tennis racket with the best of them, but a gun?

And Adelaide certainly would not inform the authorities about Addy's plan to kill his ex-wife. Mrs. Payne had been very good to her. She looked around at her elegant surroundings. And she needed Adelaide.

The man is dead. No sense telling the police about something that can't happen now.

❧TWENTY-ONE❧

"IF IT WEREN'T for all the beer signs in the window and the big 'Busch's Tavern' sign, I'd say this was a drug store," Santello said.

"It probably was twenty years ago." Shannon said and opened the door.

Santello halted inside the dim, smoky bar and sniffed. A few zombie-eyed men conversed with their drinks but weren't getting any responses. "Talk about depressing! The place even smells like dead memories."

"I think you smell the restrooms."

Santello eyed him with raised brows and nodded in agreement. They crossed to the far end of the bar and flashed their badges at a blond woman pulling some beers from the tap. "Would you mind answering a few questions?" Shannon asked.

The woman smiled nervously, looked around for someone and, not seeing that someone, shrank into herself. "I guess, but maybe you should talk to the boss."

Shannon didn't know the woman, but he recognized the type. He'd met dozens like her during his career in law enforcement. She radiated a lifetime of defeat, probably at the hands of a series of macho wiseasses who found her easy prey. He hoped they wouldn't make her day any worse than it usually was. "We'll talk to him, too. Anyone else work here?"

"No, the boss handles the night crowd."

"And the boss is?" asked Santello, her notebook open.

Emily giggled and spilled the last beer she was pulling. "Del Busch, like the name of the bar."

Santello wrote and then looked up. "Your name?"

The woman froze. "Emily Miner—e-r, not o-r."

Santello nodded.

"Ms. Miner, has Addison Payne been here recently?" Shannon asked.

She stared at him blankly. If the woman weren't so worn out, she'd probably be hyperventilating. "Addison Payne?" Recognition lit her face with a brief smile. "Uh, you mean Addy? Drives a pretty little black sports car?"

Shannon nodded. "Has he been here recently?"

Emily raised her shoulders, scrunched up her face and stared at the sports pictures on the opposite wall as if she would find the answer there. Finally, she looked at them. "Yeah, Addy comes in once in awhile."

Shannon didn't have to look at Santello to know she probably rolled her eyes at the answer. "Has he been here in the last week?"

She crossed her arms and tapped her chin, looking at the cracked ceiling for the answer. At that moment, one of the customers called to her for his beer, then a few of the others followed suit. "Just let me get these beers to them guys."

On her way back, Emily knocked at a closed door before going in. She soon came out, followed by a burly, balding man in a white, short-sleeved shirt who extended his meaty hand with a big smile but cold eyes. "Del Busch."

Shannon barely clasped the man's hand.

Busch lost his smile. "Emily tells me you want to know about Addy. He in some kind of trouble?"

"Has he been here in the last week?"

Busch nodded. "Yeah, I think he was in here sometime in the past week. Don't know which day, though." He glanced at Emily. "You remember the day?"

Eyes wide, she shook her head.

Busch went on, "Ya know, he's one of those guys makes the rounds to a lot of places. Nice enough bozo. Runs his tab up more than I like. Probably does it to all the bars. He's a drinker, not a troublemaker. Pays up when I ask him."

"Uh-huh. Did he ever take a bottle with him?"

"Don't sell bottles. Gotta watch my liquor liability."

"Did he ever have a flask he asked to have filled?"

Emily's eyes widened further as Busch raised his hands palms out. "Detective, I gotta make sure my customers don't get into trouble on account of drinking at my place. I could get a lot of grief sending them out with any liquor. No, I never seen him with a flask. Unless—" He looked hard at Emily. "Emily, you wouldn't let that guy sweet talk you into filling a flask, now would ya?"

She smiled woodenly, glancing at all of them like a bobble-headed doll. She finally locked on Busch and read the right answer on his face. "No, Del."

Busch put an arm around her shoulders. "That's my girl. Emily's one of the few helpers I've had I can trust."

"Was he friendly with any of your other customers?"

Busch glanced at a man sitting in a back booth and shook his head. "No, he drank alone. Just flirted once in awhile with Emily."

"Notice anything different about him lately?"

Busch shrugged. "I don't study these guys. I'd say Addy was the way he always was."

Emily bobbed her head in agreement.

"Thank you. Here's my card if you happen to think of anything." Shannon handed each of them a card.

Busch glanced at the card and his eyes widened. "Homicide! So if Addy ain't in trouble, why all the questions?"

"Mr. Payne is dead."

Emily yelped like a kicked puppy.

Busch went still, staring at Shannon. "Gee. That's a shame. What happened?"

"We can't comment on an ongoing investigation."

Outside on the uneven, cracked sidewalk, Santello took a deep breath. "That creep stinks worse than his bar."

"Yeah, and we're not even in Denmark."

"*Hamlet*, right? Something rotten stinks in Denmark."

Shannon grinned and nodded.

When he was sure the detectives were long gone and Busch was back in his office, Virgil scurried to the bar. He leaned in close to Emily. "Those were cops, right?"

"Yeah."

"Busch looked at me when he was talking to them. Were they looking for me?"

"No, Virgil. It wasn't about you." She sniffed and pulled a tissue out of her pocket to wipe her eyes. "Addy is dead."

"What! When?"

"I don't know, but it must've been this past week. Oh, Virgil, they was asking if he ever walked out with a bottle, or if we topped off a flask. I said 'no,' but, you know, I used to fill his flask all the time. What if . . . what if—"

"Emily, he never had a problem all them other times you did it. That guy could hold his liquor and then some. Don't beat yourself up." Virgil patted her hand. "That was last week, right? The last time?"

"Yeah, Busch just brought in a bottle of Maker's Mark from his office, Addy's favorite."

"Yeah, I saw that." Virgil smiled at her. "Don't you worry, honey. You didn't do nothing wrong." He continued patting her hand. He remembered Busch getting ready to pour the Maker's Mark into the sink after Addy left with the lock pick set—until he noticed Virgil watching him. Busch didn't fool him with that taking-a-drink-to-my-office act. Yeah, the whole deal smelled to high heaven, although Virgil wasn't sure what Busch had done.

I just hope poor little Emily don't end up holding the bag. He looked at Emily's bent head with soft eyes and caressed the hand he'd been patting. She raised her head and stared at him as if seeing him for the first time.

ᯓ᯲TWENTY–TWOᯓ᯲

"JEZEBEL! JEZEBEL, YOU naughty girl. Come!" The frail, tiny woman panicked when her little Bichon Frise failed to appear. She navigated the uneven flagstone path to the back of The Lafayette, all the while blaming herself for the dog escaping her. She had disconnected the leash only to remove Jezebel's pink shirt because of the heat. However, the feisty little minx was too quick for the arthritic woman's seventy-five years. Now she was probably in their regular dog walking area, which was off limits because of the body she and Jezebel had discovered a few days ago. Dog owners were to use the planted areas in the parking lot in front of the building for now. She hoped her little treasure wasn't licking at anything in the taped off area and shuddered at the thought.

She rounded the corner of the building, and her heart sank when she found the path and nearby grounds empty except for the fluttering police tape. Where can she be? Suddenly, she heard a familiar yelp. Turning in the direction of the sound, she saw the bantam, white ball of fur, the same white as her own hair, way down by the fence that separated the slightly sloping grounds of the co-op from the nearly sheer drop beyond. Planted shrubs and wild vines and weeds grew at the fence line to discourage dogs from digging.

Thank God, for that fence! "Jezebel! Come here!" The old lady remembered the treats in her pocket and pulled out a piece. Raising it high, she yelled, "Mommy has a treat for you." Hearing the word "treat," the small canine grabbed something shiny from the ground and gamboled up the gentle slope to her mistress. She dropped the object at her feet, sat up on her haunches, and pawed the air for her reward. The woman gave her the treat and attached the leash before Jezebel had time to beg for another. After she gave the little dog her second treat, she carefully bent down to pick up Jezebel's find.

It was a silver flask bearing the initials ATP. What was it doing in the bushes? The old lady looked back at the crime scene tape. This flask might belong to the man who fell to his death. What was his name? Addison something. But if it was his, how did it end up so far from where he fell? Somebody had to have thrown it, but she couldn't imagine why anyone would do such a thing. It might not be top of the line, but it was still too nice to discard like trash. She shook the flask and heard the slurp of liquid. As much as she loved silver and would have liked to add it to her collection, she was reared to be honest. It had to be turned in to the police. Maybe when they were through with it, they'd give it back to her.

༼༠ᚱᚱᚱ༽

"Thanks, Luissi." Shannon replaced the receiver and grinned at Santello. "The flask has a lot of smudges on it, but there were a few good prints, most of them Payne's and a few belonging to the dog owner. The others don't match up with Michaels' or any of the other people we printed. And . . ."

"And?" prompted Santello.

Shannon trumpeted a riff with his lips "Ladies and Gentlemen, the flask contained alcohol and traces of the drug, amphetamine."

"What a break!"

"Yeah, now we can tell Michaels she's no longer under suspicion."

Santello rolled back in her chair. "Let's not get ahead of ourselves, Shannon. She's a smart lady. She'd wear gloves."

Shannon gave her the stink eye.

"I'm just saying it's too early in the game to be eliminating suspects. Don't forget the Kernans also had keys to Michaels' place. We know Mr. Kernan was in New York for a few days and in flight when Payne died. We still don't know where Mrs. Kernan was."

"Okay, okay. I think we should send Forensics out to see if there's anything else they can find along that fence. If Payne threw that flask out there, who knows what else might be out there?"

"Oh, my cousin's going to love us for having him pick through that little jungle."

"Aw, Luissi will just make the others do it and supervise every move they make." Shannon called Luissi and made the arrangements. He turned to Santello. "What do you say we get prints from Del Busch and Emily Miner?"

"I'm with you. Think we can get them without their knowing it? It'd be so much faster if we didn't have to wait for a warrant."

"Worth a try. We'll take a glossy six pack page of 'suspects' for them to look at—two, so each of them only handles one page," Shannon said. He slung his arms into the sleeves of his jacket. "Might as well make Luissi's life easier."

"I like the way you think. Let's go."

ᘒᢗᢔᢓᢒ

"It's Luissi," mouthed Santello, her hand covering the mouthpiece of the phone.

Shannon nodded and waited.

"Uh-huh. . . . Uh-huh. . . . Yeah?" Her eyes widened, then crinkled. "Good. . . . Right back at ya, Luissi." Hanging up, she looked at Shannon like a dog that had emptied the cat's dish without getting caught. Striking the desk with her fist, she yelled, "Bingo! Luissi said they found a lock pick set caught on the fence behind some bushes."

Shannon grinned. "Now we know how he got in."

"If they're his. Luissi said they're standard police issue. A-a-a-and . . . drum roll, please."

Shannon grabbed two pens and beat a tattoo on the desk.

"The prints on the flask are Emily Miner's." To her surprise, Shannon was no longer smiling. "Why so glum?"

He dropped the pens onto the desk and slumped back in his chair. "I was hoping it was Busch. That woman looks like she's never had a good day."

"Yeah, well, maybe she finally had way too many bad days."

"What do you mean?"

Across the aisle, Korpielsky and a second detective knew what was coming. They sat back and readied themselves for another Santello performance.

Santello looked at Shannon like he wasn't exactly the sharpest hoe in the garden shed. "Rejection."

"Huh?"

One of the detectives—Shannon couldn't tell which—stifled a snicker.

"Look, Seamus Aloysius, Payne drives up in a shiny black Jaguar, strolls in wearing tailored suits, and orders Maker's Mark. He flirts with her a little. Isn't that what salesmen do?"

Shannon shrugged. The other detectives nodded.

Santello paced back and forth, while her hands punctuated her words. "So, she says to herself, 'I wouldn't kick this one out of my bed.' Every time he comes in, she starts dreaming—dinners at fancy restaurants, dancing in ritzy nightclubs, waking up the next morning in his penthouse, cooking him breakfast while wearing one of his tailored shirts. Problem is, Prince Charming doesn't even offer her a ride in his fancy coach let alone ask her out. When he leaves the bar with only a smile and maybe a wave, she feels like she's been had. She gets angry. She wants to punish him. So what does she do? She crushes some diet pills and doctors the liquor. Maybe she didn't intend for him to die, but she wanted him to suffer after drinking that expensive stuff. Oh yeah, she was going to show him, all right."

The other two detectives shook their heads and laughed. Shannon doubled over and hooted. "Santello, you have one hell of an imagination. I'll give you that. Thing is, Squires said Payne had to have taken a huge dose of the stimulant. There wouldn't have been enough amphetamine in diet pills to account for the amount in his system."

"Imagination, my Uncle Luigi's homemade grappa! It fits! She could've bought the stuff on the street. It's pretty easy to find."

"Be honest. Can you see that timid little woman having the gumption to follow through on a plan like that? Weren't you just as sure that Michaels pushed him off her terrace?"

"Yeah, well, little Miss Timid maybe isn't so timid, and Michaels still could've done it."

"Santello, he got in with a lock pick."

"If the pick was his. . . . Well, even if he picked the lock, Michaels or any one of her friends could've been there anyway."

He rolled his eyes. "It was the amphetamine combined with the liquor that caused the aneurysm that killed him."

Hands on hips, she said, "So? They had motive. I'm just saying we shouldn't cross those scenarios off the list yet."

Shannon shook his head.

Santello grinned broadly. "So let's get an arrest warrant for the Miner woman. The DA could make a case for manslaughter or at least reckless endangerment." She rubbed her hands together. "I just gotta arrest somebody. And we'll make the DA so-o-o happy."

"It's all circumstantial. That liquor could have been doctored by someone else."

"Like who? Michaels? Mrs. Kernan?"

Shannon grimaced. "Maybe Payne's building super. Except I don't know what his motive might be. I still like Busch for the deed."

Santello regarded him with the innocence of a preschooler. "But he's such an upstanding citizen."

He looked at her stone-faced with one eyebrow arched. That look told her it was time she shut up. So she crossed her arms and waited.

He sighed and picked up the phone to call the DA's office. "Okay, let's get that warrant. If nothing else, maybe it'll shake some bananas out of the tree."

Santello spun around, arms held high. "Yes, we have no bananas. . . ." She continued what she could remember of the old song, egged on by the cheers and clapping of the other two detectives until Shannon shushed her.

Virgil entered Busch's and nearly stumbled back out of the door of the tavern when Emily crashed into him. Her elbow felt like a pointy stick jabbing him in the gut. The two detectives from the other day rushed up behind her. Virgil grabbed her by the shoulders and looked into her tear-stained, red face. "Whoa, Emily, what's the matter?"

"Ms. Miner, please, we have to take you in. Don't make it worse by resisting," the woman detective said. "You've been read your rights, and you can have a lawyer." The woman cuffed Emily's hands behind her.

"What's with the handcuffs? Virgil said.

"What does it look like? We're arresting her," the woman detective said.

"You arresting Emily? Why? Emily wouldn't do nothing bad."

"I didn't do it!" Emily mewed, squirming against the cuffs.

"Of course, you didn't, honey." He turned to the detectives as though he were taking charge. "What's going on here?"

Before either of the detectives could answer, Emily cried out, "They think I drugged Addy's flask . . . that I killed him! I told them I couldn't do nothing like that. I kept telling them, but they . . ." Her eyes rolled up in her head and she slumped to the floor. The detectives coaxed her back to consciousness and stood her on her feet.

Virgil grasped her shoulders again. "Where's Busch?"

"He went to the bank. Oh God, Virgil, do you think he'll fire me?"

He looked around and found the place empty. He let go of her and drew the male detective aside. "Look, Officer—"

"Detective Shannon."

"Yeah, Detective. Emily wouldn't do nothing like that. She really dug the guy. Let him run a tab and filled his flask with the good stuff for free. You should be arresting Busch.

"Ms. Miner's prints were the ones on Mr. Payne's flask."

"Yeah, I know." Virgil glance at Emily and then back at Shannon. "What else I know is Busch don't let no one get the best of him. You cross him, and he's gonna get ya sooner or later. I got personal experience with that."

"Yeah, he seems like that kind of guy. So how do you figure him for this?"

"Look, I'm here every day after work. I see a lot." He jerked his head at the bar. "You see that bottle of Maker's Mark on the shelf?"

Shannon nodded.

"Addy's the only one ever asked for it. Busch didn't even stock it until Addy started coming round." He glanced back at Emily who was now perched on the edge of a chair with her head down and the woman detective, arms crossed, sitting next to her. He walked Shannon further away from them. "I remember that last time Addy was here. There weren't no Maker's Mark on that shelf. Then I seen Busch bring in the bottle, and when Busch went back to his office, Emily topped off Addy's flask with it."

"So you'll testify to that?"

Virgil frowned and shook his head. "It don't mean Emily done it. What I'm saying is Busch poisoned him."

"That's your opinion. He's not exactly the nicest guy around, but—"

"I bet I can prove it." He pointed to the Maker's Mark on the shelf. "See, that bottle there ain't the first one Busch brung in."

"I don't follow."

"Okay, back then, I couldn't make out what he was doing. But when Emily told me Addy was dead, I pieced it together. See, I seen Busch getting ready to pour the Maker's Mark into the sink after Addy left. I know it was the same bottle Emily used to top off Addy's flask. When he seen me looking at him, Busch stopped what he was doing. Then he capped the bottle, grabbed a glass, and went back to his office like he was gonna have a little drink in private. A little later, I seen him come out with a bottle and put it back on the shelf. He looked at me like he knew I was watching."

"So?"

"So, I don't think it's the same bottle. I bet the only fingerprints on that bottle are Busch's. Maybe the seal's not even broke. Can't tell from here. 'Cept I think Busch's too smart to let that get by him. Emily can tell you if anyone's asked for it 'cept Addy. That time was the last time Addy was here, and Emily's never been what you'd call the perfect housekeeper. It's been sitting there all this time, and no one's probably touched it. Besides, I'll bet you a fin, there ain't no drugs in it."

Shannon stared at Virgil. "She could have added the drug to the flask."

Virgil chuckled and shook his head. "Too many eyes. Emily's all thumbs, would've fumbled the whole deal. Anyway, I seen her pour the booze straight from the bottle—the first bottle, that is. Who knows where that one got to?" He pointed to the Maker's Mark on the shelf. "You check that bottle. You'll see."

Virgil could see the beginning of a smile on Shannon's face as the detective went behind the bar and used a napkin to pick up the bottle and place it in a paper bag he'd found under the counter. He sealed the bag with some tape and labeled it appropriately. Virgil wondered if the guy had been playing dumb just to get him to talk.

"Santello, I've written a receipt to Mr. Busch for one bottle of Maker's Mark." He glanced up at Virgil. "I'm leaving the receipt right here by the cash register."

"Okay, Shannon. Can we get going before we have to carry this lady out to the car?"

"In a minute." Shannon flipped to a fresh page in his notebook. "Your name, address, and contact information?"

"Sure. By the way, I'm a janitor at the local precinct. Took a vacation day today to take care of some business. The desk sergeant can vouch for me." Virgil called over to Emily, "Don't you worry, honey. Everything's going to be alright." Then he turned back to Shannon. "Name's Virgil Earp."

"'Virgil Earp' as in—"

Virgil always enjoyed the reaction to his name. "Yeah, as in, but no relation to them Earps out West, although Dad's folks come from there. Mom thought it'd be cute and point me in the right direction. She wanted to call me Wyatt, but Dad said the kids would tease the hell outta me. So they named me after Wyatt's brother."

Busch stood open-mouthed in front of his tavern. Not yet two o'clock and the closed sign's on! What the hell is that broad up to? Only been gone a little while, and she's screwing up my business! He thrust the door open, slamming it against the wall, and found Virgil draped on a stool at the bar, nursing a drink. Otherwise the place was as empty as a church at two in the morning. "What are you doing here so early? Where's Emily? What the hell's with the closed sign?"

Virgil sipped his drink and placed it on the bar before answering. "She's in jail."

Busch belly laughed. "That's rich. Come on, Virgil. What is it? That time of the month, and she had to go home because her tummy hurt?"

Virgil grabbed a swizzle stick and offered it to Busch. "Here, clean your ears out. I said she's in jail. Those detectives who was here before arrested her and asked me to stay here 'til you got back. Since I'm a janitor at the precinct, they figured they could trust me."

Busch growled and made a fist at Virgil. "Yeah, if they only knew."

"If you'd left the key, they could have locked up for you."

"Why'd they—"

The phone rang. Virgil went back to enjoying his drink.

Busch grabbed the phone. "Yeah. . . . This is Del Busch. . . . Yeah, I just heard. I can tell you, whatever it is you think she done, she's too dumb to do it. . . . What do you mean, she drugged Payne?" He caught his breath and then bristled. "You know, I got a business to run. I can't just— Okay, okay!" Busch rolled his eyes. "Yeah, I know where you're at!"

Tight-lipped, Busch slammed down the phone. He smirked at Virgil. "Detective Shannon would appreciate it if I would come in and answer a few questions to—how did he put it? Oh, yeah—'to corroborate Emily's story.'"

Virgil nodded and looked wide-eyed at Busch. "Really?"

Busch grabbed Virgil and snarled at him. "Get your ass the hell outta here!"

"But I ain't finished my drink!" Virgil waved Shannon's receipt at Busch. "And they left—"

Busch shoved him toward the door and the receipt flew out of Virgil's hand and floated to the floor.

"It probably ain't the only one you had. Be happy I ain't charging you for it." Busch banged out the door after him and locked up.

⋟⋞TWENTY-THREE⋟⋞

"DON'T NEED THE tape recorder," Shannon said and handed it back to Santello outside the interrogation room.

"Shannon? Is this why your fellow MP's in Nam called you 'The Wing Man'?"

Shannon answered with a smile. Santello raised her eyes to the heavens she could not see through the soundproof ceiling tiles and opened the door to the room on the other side of the two-way mirror, which was already occupied by an assistant district attorney.

Light filtering from the dirt-clouded window and the single forty-watt bulb in the ceiling barely illuminated the interrogation room Shannon entered. Because he'd turned off the AC unit in the room, the vague odor of urine and pine disinfectant permeated the humid air as the room heated up. A scarred, narrow wood table and four wood chairs occupied the nine by nine. It was purposely the worst of the three nine by nines, intended for the toughest suspects. "Sorry to keep you waiting, Mr. Busch."

Busch was not wearing his happy face. "I been sitting here almost an hour. I got a business to run, you know."

Shannon took the chair opposite him. Busch drummed the pads of his fingers on the table. Sweat beaded his forehead and formed gray, wet patches under his arms. Shannon opened the file folder and paged through it. He tapped his pen in counterpoint to Busch's drumming. After a moment, he stopped tapping and looked up.

A tic pulsed below Busch's left eye. Shannon smiled at him. "I really do appreciate your coming in to help us out with this."

"Yeah, yeah. Let's get this over with. Maybe I can get back in time to open for the evening crowd."

Would you like some water? Coffee?"

"No! Just ask your questions so I can get outta here."

"Okay." Shannon looked down at a sheet of paper in the folder. "According to Ms. Miner's statement, the last time Mr. Payne visited your establishment, she topped off his flask with Maker's Mark."

Busch stared at Shannon. "What? She what! I didn't know nothing about that. I can't believe she would do that to me! That stuff's expensive." He crossed his arms. "She ain't working for me no more!"

"According to her statement, you did know and took the tip Mr. Payne gave her . . . and docked her a week's pay."

Busch reddened and slapped the table with both hands. "That lying bitch! She's been robbing me blind. Now she's trying—" He tightened his mouth and looked away from Shannon.

"Trying what, Mr. Busch?"

He turned back to Shannon and stuck his chin out. "She's lying! That's what! She's up to her neck in it all, and she's telling you whatever story she thinks will get her out of it!"

Shannon nodded. "Must be hard to find good help." Then he looked up at Busch. "Especially honest help. . . . Does Ms. Miner have a drug problem? Maybe a little speed to keep her going?"

Busch crossed his arms like he was hugging himself. "How the hell should I know?"

Protective posture—good. "How about you, Mr. Busch? You seem to be at your tavern a lot. Maybe a little pharmaceutical help keeps you going."

"I resent that! I don't do drugs. Don't let no dopers into my place either."

"But you know who the local dopers are?"

"They ain't hard to spot."

Shannon nodded and turned to another page.

Busch wiped his face and settled back into his chair. "Uh, hey, what's this drug stuff about?"

He looked up at Busch. "Mr. Payne died from a thoracic aortic aneurysm."

"A what? *Post-Gazette* said he fell off a building."

"Yes, he did. But he was dead before he hit the ground. You see, Mr. Busch, his aortic artery had thinned over time and bulged out. That's what's called an aortic aneurysm. The aortic artery is the major artery from the heart. The day Mr. Payne died, that bulge blew out and killed him instantly— maybe he didn't even know what was happening to him. Coroner says a combination of alcohol and amphetamine triggered the burst aneurysm."

Nodding, Busch regarded Shannon through slitted eyes. "So you think Emily sold him some dope?"

Shannon shrugged and lifted his eyebrows.

"Well, you sure as hell don't think I did?"

Shannon shrugged again. "I don't know what to think. Coroner says there weren't any pills in Payne's stomach. He said the amphetamine had to be dissolved in the liquor."

"Yeah?"

"Yeah. And Mr. Payne's flask contained alcohol generously laced with amphetamine. So you see where this leads us?"

"No. I don't." But Busch, arms still wrapped tight around himself, was nodding and rocking as though he did see.

"Well, let me explain. Ms. Miner's prints are on the flask, which means she handled it, and she readily admits she filled it with Maker's Mark. However, she denies adding anything to the whiskey. She also says the Maker's Mark wasn't on the shelf until you brought it out right before Mr. Payne left."

Busch rocked his head from side to side. "Nah, nah, nah. She's lying again."

Shannon remained silent.

"Course, she's such a ditzy broad, she probably didn't see it until I walked by and thought I just brung it."

"Hm." Shannon, his eyebrows drawn together, stared at the wall behind Busch.

Busch pulled out a crumpled hanky and wiped his face. "Your AC broke?" He wrinkled his nose. "You'ns could do a better job of cleaning this place."

Shannon rested his arms on the table and leaned forward as though he were sharing privileged information. "You know, Mr. Busch, when we arrested Ms. Miner, we brought in the bottle of Maker's Mark for testing." At Busch's concerned look, he said, "Oh, we left you a receipt by the cash register. Didn't you see it? The Department will reimburse you for the bottle."

Busch's expression did not change.

Shannon sighed and pulled back. "However, that bottle created more questions than it answered. You see, the seal was broken, and some of the liquor was gone, but the only fingerprints on the bottle were yours. Oh, and it was just Maker's Mark in the bottle. No drugs."

"Well, there you go. Emily must've drugged Payne's flask." A bead of sweat traveled down Busch's nose, landing on his shirt.

"But if it's the same bottle she used to top off Payne's flask, why aren't her fingerprints on it?"

"She could've wiped the bottle. Sometimes they drip."

"And not even smear your prints?"

Busch shrugged and smiled weakly. "Well, I'm not sure, but could be I replaced the bottle when the other one was empty."

"A lot of folks must've been ordering Maker's Mark over the past week. I didn't realize your regular clientele could afford it? Ms. Miner said that a little more than two thirds of the whiskey was left, and the last one to order it was Mr. Payne."

"Detective, she ain't that bright. Or, like I was saying, she's lying." Busch swiped his hanky across his face again. "Look, Detective, I need to get back to my business."

"Uh-huh." Shannon closed the file and folded his hands together on the table. He leaned into Busch, his chilly blue eyes trained on Busch's brown ones. "Mr. Busch, I don't for one minute believe Ms. Miner is as dumb as you make her out to be. And she has the kind of face that'd make her a lousy poker player."

Busch cleared his throat and looked away from Shannon.

"Look at me, Mr. Busch!"

He swept his eyes back to Shannon.

"This is what I think happened. You found out that Ms. Miner was topping off Payne's flask every time he came in. And with your best liquor. Part of what tipped you off was that the bottle was going faster than usual, yet Payne's tab didn't seem to add up. That got you angry. You watched. When you saw it happening with your own eyes, and that he was tipping Ms. Miner to boot, you really got pissed. Here was this down-on-his-luck rich boy making a fool out of you. But nobody pulls Del Busch's tail, right?"

Busch reddened and tightened his lips, looking away from Shannon.

"I want to see your eyes, Del! Now!"

Busch clenched his fists and fixed Shannon with dark, hooded eyes.

"So you decided to get back at Payne. The easiest way would be to doctor his drink with a little dope. Barbiturates might cause him to kill someone while he was driving, but speed? Oh, yeah. That would really screw him up but probably not cause any accidents. Lucky thing his heart didn't give out while he was driving. Who knows how many people he would've taken out?"

"I told you I don't have nothing to do with dope or them junkies in the neighborhood," he said through tightly clamped teeth.

Shannon rushed on. "Junkies in the neighborhood? Hell, you probably know them all by name. Vice can shake down a few of them to find out who sold it to you. Cops are real good at negotiating. Think any of those junkies care to protect you?"

Busch glared and said nothing.

"Now, what I think you did then was to make sure you had two bottles of Maker's Mark. One you doctored with amphetamine. You kept neither on the shelf behind the bar. You waited until Payne paid a visit. Ms. Miner swears there was no Maker's Mark on the shelf or in the storage room before you came out of your office. She thought nothing of it when you came out with the bottle. Figured you were having a little toot of the good stuff in your office. When you returned to your office, she topped off Mr. Payne's flask.

When he left, you sent her off to clean the bathrooms. Then, with nobody paying any attention to you, you grabbed the bottle and a glass and headed back to your office, the picture of the boss enjoying some of the good stuff in private. Sometime later, you placed a new bottle on the shelf. Thing is, only your prints are on that bottle, no smudges, just your prints. I wonder where the original bottle is—nowhere near your place, I bet."

Busch growled, looking like he was going to lunge at Shannon. "That prissy *Hahvahd* Business School bastard always walked into my place like he was some kind of prince, like he was better than everyone else—better than me. He'd act like we was the same, but I could see he was laughing behind his eyes—like I was too stupid to notice. After awhile, I didn't bother too much with him. But I could see he got to

Emily, so I'd watch once in awhile. She's a dumb, easy broad. Didn't want her giving away the whole kit and caboodle. Yeah. It's like you said. I was pissed, and I was gonna fix him— make sure he never came back to my place again. But I just wanted to mess him up a little. I didn't want to kill the bozo."

"Why didn't you just bar him from your tavern?"

Busch smiled. "No fun in that. I wanted him to be sick, to know that I was on to him, and that this blue-collar tavern owner wasn't as dumb as he thought. I wanted to humiliate the bastard! But I never figured the dope'd kill him."

Shannon read Busch his rights, pulled out a yellow note pad, and shoved it toward him along with a pen. "Remember I said we were good at negotiating?"

Busch nodded.

"Well, you write down everything you did and why, sign and date it, and I'll see what we can work out with the District Attorney." Shannon smiled. "After all, you never intended to kill Mr. Payne, right?"

Focused on writing his confession, Busch shook his head.

"You want to call your lawyer, Del?" Shannon asked one more time.

Busch smirked, shook his head again, and continued writing.

"Is that a 'no'?"

"No. I don't want no shyster lawyer." His eyes never left the note pad.

On the other side of the two-way mirror, two people deflated with a sigh. The assistant DA rubbed his bald pate. "It's a good thing he got the guy to write a confession. I was ready to leave when he walked in without a tape recorder and didn't even bother to read the guy his rights. By the way, did you get a search warrant for that place?"

"No, just an arrest warrant," Santello said. "If we'd have waited to get a search warrant after we found out about the bottle, Busch might have come back and done away with it."

"Then it's really a good thing he got him to write that confession. No way could we have used the Maker's Mark bottle as evidence. We can probably do a plea bargain and avoid a court trial. Less chance of him wiggling out of the charges."

Santello folded her arms and smiled. "You know, I like Shannon to believe I don't think he's too smart, but," she nodded at the scene beyond the mirror, "that's the reason none of us play poker with him anymore."

"Wouldn't want to be Busch's lawyer."

Santello's eyes twinkled. "Yeah, poor guy loses two ways—no real defense and a pissy client to work with. I just love finding the perps and kicking their asses. Makes my day."

The assistant DA nodded at her and grinned.

⟨⟨⟩⟩

The two detectives strolled to their desks.

"Way to go, you two! What do you say we go to Mahoney's to celebrate?" Korpielsky called out.

"Sounds good," Santello answered. Korpielsky's phone rang and he turned to answer it. Grinning widely, she turned to Shannon. "I'm glad you cleaned up after that interview. Phew! How did you stand it in there?"

"Ah, the things we do to serve justice."

"By the way, your dinner? My treat."

He slumped into his chair. "What, Santello? No 'Seamus Aloysius, you almost screwed up'?"

"Hey, I'll give you this one. Better keep on your toes from now on, though."

Shannon laughed. "Thanks for the dinner offer, but I'll only be at Mahoney's long enough for a beer or two. I'm going over to Ms. Michaels to tell her the good news."

She narrowed her eyes. "Couldn't you just phone her?"

Eyes twinkling, Shannon grinned at her.

Santello stared back, wide-eyed. "So, you didn't just scrub the stink away for your fellow peace officers, huh?" She grinned. "Hey, I'd like to be part of the good news delegation, too. Mind if I come along?"

"Thought you didn't much like her?"

"Well, that's when I thought she killed Payne. I couldn't figure out how he got into her place. Figured she or one of her friends let him in. I was pulling your leg before when I was going on about how she or a friend still could have pushed him, but finding the lock picks clinched it for me. What I don't get is what he was doing at her place. And why did he pitch the lock pick set and that fancy flask of his into those bushes?"

"There was nothing missing from her apartment, so burglary wasn't a motive. Why he threw out the flask, we'll never know. The lock picks, though—he probably didn't want them on him in case he got stopped by one of our finest."

"He must've really wanted something pretty bad to go to all the trouble of sneaking into her place. Lock pick sets are pretty expensive for someone down on his luck, and they're pretty easy to trace."

Shannon smiled at her as though he'd solved the riddle of which came first in the chicken or egg controversy.

"What?"

"That particular set is standard equipment at all the Pittsburgh precincts. Have we met anyone who works at a precinct and also frequents Busch's Tavern?"

Santello gasped. "No! Not Virgil Earp! But he's the one put us on the right track."

"That he did. But he never admitted to any involvement with Payne."

"Gee, he even came down here to pick up Ms. Miner. The desk sergeant said he came in no more than five minutes after Busch. Waited all that time for her to be released, too."

"Guess she could do worse."

"But he's a thief! We need to report him to his precinct."

"He'll make a better witness without a record if Busch doesn't plead out, and the case goes to court." Shannon grinned. "Maybe he'll give up his crooked ways for Ms. Miner. He did come to her rescue."

Santello rocked her head side to side and grimaced. "Well, I guess nobody's perfect. Sooner or later he'll get caught if he keeps swiping city property."

Shannon got up and slipped into his jacket. Santello grabbed her purse. They exited the squad room, and she grinned at him. "Well, Shannon, I'm not going to get in your way. This time you get the girl—but if you screw up, well. . . ."

"Yeah, we'll see."

⚜TWENTY–FOUR⚜

SHANNON HOPED THE breath spray would overcome the beer breath. The tactic never did fool his mother when he was a kid. However, he'd finished belching long before hc left Mahoney's, so a little minty beer breath shouldn't be too offensive, although it didn't do much for the taste in his mouth. Sniffing at his underarms, he was glad he'd showered and changed clothes at the station. He took one last look in the rearview mirror, ran the comb through his neatly-styled curly hair a third time, and got out of his car.

He flashed his badge at the concierge and soon found himself standing before her doors. He pressed the bell. It occurred to him she might not be there, might have gone out to dinner with some friends. After all, it was nearly seven o'clock. As he pondered the possibility that she might even be out on a date, the door opened, releasing the strains of Stravinsky's *Rite of Spring*. He was momentarily stunned by the sight of her as well as the aroma of rosemary and roasting chicken. The cooking smells almost triggered a growl from a stomach digesting beer and pretzels.

"So where are the handcuffs, Detective?"

Shannon smiled and shook his head.

"Come in. The concierge alerted me you were on your way up."

He followed her down the steps to the living room and sat. "Am I interrupting your dinner?"

"No. The chicken needs a little more time," she said and removed the white chef's apron she wore over jeans and a long white shirt. "So, you have news?"

"Yes. We found the person who doctored Mr. Payne's liquor."

"Thank God! I didn't think this would ever end."

"We believe your ex-husband lost consciousness standing on that bench and fell because of the aneurysm. We have no reason to believe he was pushed. He could have died at any time that day." He told her the whole story.

"You know, I did see something glittering down by the fence the night I got back into my place, but then I forgot all about it. Clever little dog, that Jezebel."

"Yes, she elevated my opinion of tiny dogs."

I can't tell you what a relief it is to be finally cleared. It's been awful having that suspicion hanging over my head. Some people who don't know me very well have been looking at me differently lately. That's not the worst of it though. The hint of scandal has affected our business as well. We've been negotiating the purchase of another publishing company, and although the owner has known me since I worked at the Kernan's print shop, he's very protective of his company's reputation. So he's delaying the sale until all this blows over. Now that I'm in the clear, we can proceed with the purchase."

"I'm sorry about that. The story should be on the eleven o'clock news tonight and in tomorrow's paper."

Smiling, she gazed out at the terrace and became somber. She shook her head.

"What is it?" he asked.

"What was Addy doing here?"

"We've been wondering the same thing. . . . Oh, by the way, Detective Santello wanted me to apologize for any discomfort we may have caused you."

Liz pursed her lips. "You mean any discomfort *she* caused me. I suspect that's why she's not here, Detective."

"Oh, she wanted to come, but she had to take her mother and grandmother to bingo." It was just a little white lie. "The investigation is closed, so this is really an unofficial visit. 'Detective' seems so formal. Please, call me 'Jim.'"

She nodded curtly. "You may call me 'Ms. Michaels.'"

He looked like a man who had burped in the face of Queen Elizabeth.

She laughed. "Liz. Call me 'Liz.'"

He smiled back, shaking his head, and returned to the mystery of why Payne had broken into her place. "Like I said, we've been trying to figure out why Mr. Payne was here. We know he took nothing." He stopped smiling when an idea occurred to him. "Would he have physically forced you to give him the money he wanted? Was he ever violent with you during your marriage?"

"I'm not the kind of woman who would tolerate physical abuse. In fact, I don't tolerate emotional abuse. I'm not a needy woman."

"Yes, I could tell that, right off the bat." Shannon hesitated a moment. "This may be far-fetched. But would he have benefitted from your death?"

"No. He's not in my will. He had to know that, and the only life insurance policy on me is carried by the company. It benefits the business in the event of my death. There is similar coverage on the Kernans as well."

"Hm." Shannon nodded. "We did visit his apartment, but his mother had taken all of his personal effects. So we have no idea if he had a life insurance policy on you."

Liz shook her head. "I seriously doubt he could afford the premium for a substantial amount, unless he used some of the money from the sale of the house. But I'm sure most of that money went to increase the profits of the liquor industry." She sighed. "I guess we'll never know why he was here."

"Could he have wanted to talk you into taking him back?"

Liz laughed. "If that's why he was here, then he was truly delusional. Besides, breaking into my home to persuade me to take him back would not have endeared him to me."

"Well, I thought that, too, but people, especially drunks, aren't always logical."

A timer in the kitchen dinged.

"I guess that's my cue to leave. Enjoy your dinner, Liz. It smells delicious."

As they both got up, she said, "De—Jim?"

He turned to her and his pulse quickened. "Yes?"

"Would you like to join me for dinner? I mean, the investigation is closed, and since I'm no longer a suspect, you don't have to worry about me poisoning you."

Shannon grinned broadly. "Yes, I would—I mean, I'd like to join you for dinner—not that I would worry about you poisoning me."

"Please," she said and directed him to the dining room. "I'll set another place and bring in the food."

"Would you like any help?"

"No." She turned and smiled. "But it's very nice of you to offer."

"My mother and four sisters trained me well." He looked at the formal setting as he took his seat. "Do you always set your table with linen and candles?"

"Yes. I consider food a celebration deserving all the fanfare of a formal dinner. After all, some living creature died so I might eat. I believe Native Americans give thanks to the animals they kill. The least I can do is to cook the creature to the best of my ability and honor it with my best setting."

"I guess that's because of the way you were brought up."

Liz paused and smiled to herself. "Yes. Yes, I suppose you could say it's because of the way I was brought up."

Shannon enjoyed the salad of greens in a vinaigrette dressing, chicken, asparagus with Hollandaise, garlic roasted potatoes, and crusty French bread so much that he accepted a second helping of everything except the salad. He marveled at the medley of flavors and asked how she prepared the chicken and roasted potatoes. She reluctantly parted with the information, but he had the feeling she wasn't telling him everything that would be necessary to produce the same results.

He sipped his wine. "Do you always cook so much? Seems like a lot of food for one person. Would you have eaten all of this if I hadn't shown up?"

Liz laughed. "No. I like to freeze meals for times when I'm just too tired to prepare a meal the way it deserves."

"Freeze food like this?"

"I know, but I have my ways."

They talked about food, places where Liz found the best produce and meats, and reasonably-priced restaurants that served well-prepared fare. She enjoyed going to the different ethnic bazaars the churches throughout the city often held and sampling dishes made from recipes brought from the old country. They had pretty much exhausted movies, and she told him about the recent productions at the Pittsburgh Playhouse.

Shannon hadn't been to the Playhouse since before he went into the service. Truth be told, he hadn't been much of anywhere since Angie died, except when Eileen dragged him somewhere when no one else would go with her. And that wasn't all that often.

Neither spoke of dead spouses or lost babies. Nor did they talk much about their respective families. Shannon sensed she was a very private person, not one to blather her entire life story to a stranger. He recalled some basic details from the background check he'd glanced at, but personal histories would have to be eased into in time, that is, if there was to be time for the two of them down the road. He hoped so. For the first time since Angie's death, he'd discovered a woman he really wanted to get to know. Angie would have liked her.

"It's really not important to the investigation now," he said, "but where was Mrs. Kernan the afternoon of Payne's death? It's been driving Santello nuts."

"I suppose I can tell you now, but promise me you'll keep it from your partner for a little longer."

He grinned. "Okay."

"Miriam is a concentration camp survivor. She was able to identify a rather brutal guard from the camp where she was confined and confirm what he'd done. That afternoon, she provided an affidavit to the group who would be taking him to Israel for trial. She couldn't say anything until they were out of the country."

The candles had burned down half of their length, and he realized he would soon have to leave. When she stood to clear the table, he did, too. He really didn't want the evening to end. There was so much to like in this woman beyond her physical beauty. She had a warmth, humor, and depth to her that enhanced the beauty which could be seen as icy by less discerning eyes. He hoped he'd have a chance to explore those depths. This woman would never be boring, and he felt at home with her.

He knew it was quirky of him, but he really liked that she had done nothing to correct the space between her teeth despite everything else she had done to enhance her appearance and life. That gap in her teeth reminded him of Paddy's, but Paddy couldn't wait to save enough money to have his corrected. That space also reminded him of his dead brother-in-law, Ivy. Come to think of it, Liz had that same slenderness and fairness. He wondered if she had some Swedish in her, too.

She eyed him as she loaded the dishwasher. He grinned when her back was turned. Hm. I think the interest is mutual.

"You know, I don't do the cooking at my sister's, so you'll have to let me return the favor with dinner out."

Liz brightened. "I think I'd like that. What do you have in mind?"

"You said you've never been to O'Rourke's. Would you like to try some really good authentic Irish food?"

"I'm game."

"How does Friday work for you? Say I pick you up around six?"

"I'll be ready."

Shannon paused a moment at the door, and then smiled and nodded his goodbye.

॰⟨✦⟩॰

Liz had no sooner closed the door behind Shannon than she spied her mother and grandmother. The scent of vanilla competed with the fading aroma of rosemary chicken. Both were smiling broadly.

"Oh, what are you two grinning about, anyway?"

As usual, they disappeared without answering, but Liz could swear she heard the echo of light laughter fading along with the scent of vanilla.

ꙮTWENTY-FIVEꙮ

"PRETTY LATE TONIGHT, Jimmy, aren't you?" Eileen removed her glasses and rested her open book on her lap.

Shannon was pleased to see her reading instead of fussing around the house. With Paddy living in the dorm, she now had more time for her favorite pastime. He smiled at his oldest sister, sitting in what was once Ivy's Naugahyde recliner. She looked pretty good for a woman in her late fifties—still slender, a few strands of gray peeking from her long dark waves, and reading glasses perched on her thin nose.

She could have remarried after Ivy died. There had been quite a crowd of widowers and bachelors vying for her attention. She still got calls and a visit now and then from interested men. Of course, very few of them deserved his sister's attention. In the past, he'd even noticed Ivy gazing at her at times as though he couldn't believe this extraordinary creature was his wife. She seemed content with her life as it was. "Wasn't all work, Ei."

"Glad to hear it. If you're hungry, there are leftovers in the fridge." She stared at him a moment. "You look a little different." Her eyes crinkled when she smiled. "You met somebody, didn't you?"

Hands on hips, he looked at her open-mouthed. "How do you do that?"

She laughed. "You're my baby brother, Jimmy. I know what you're thinking even before you think it. So tell me about her."

Shannon frowned and shook his head. "Ei, I don't know if I want to talk about it right now. How about we give it some time to see how things go?"

When she stopped smiling, he said, "Tell you what, I promise to tell you all about her if it gets to the point where I want to introduce her to the family. And speaking of the family, please don't tell them I'm seeing someone. I don't want to run the gauntlet of questions again like I had to when I dated Lisa."

Eileen smirked. "Well, it was pretty amusing watching you run that gauntlet."

He eyed her.

"Okay, Jimmy, okay. Mum's the word." She replaced her glasses and picked up her book.

Shannon yawned and stretched. "I'm going to bed."

"Pleasant dreams, Jimmy."

She chuckled as he left the room.

Eileen nestled deeper into the recliner and gazed beyond the book in her hands. She hoped her brother would find love again. This woman, whoever she was, had caught his eye. Perhaps she was the one.

Jimmy had grieved so deeply when Angie died, Eileen wondered if there might ever be another woman who could rekindle the spark he'd lost. There had been no one who could do that for her; however, she had her family. But Jimmy? Oh, no, please, not for him the life of the lonely, old bachelor uncle of the family. He deserved so much more; he had so much to give.

He had dated a nice enough woman from their church, but Eileen had seen no fireworks between them. Neither did anyone else in the family. There was something different here, though. She could almost smell it. Her children called it her psychic sense, but she knew it wasn't—not like the way her cousin Brigit was gifted. Eileen believed her own sense was based on observation of human behavior, well developed because she had been the oldest in a large family and had reared four children of her own. She could even read Ivy when others had no clue what he was thinking.

Ivy. When he was sick, she had sometimes caught him with a wistful, sad, faraway look in his eyes and suspected there might be a secret in his past he had not yet shared with her. She believed he would explain himself in time, but his weak heart took him before he could. After Ivy died, she discovered what that secret was. Brigit had said that she saw five children in one of her prophetic dreams about them when Eileen was pregnant with their first, but Paddy had been their fourth and last child. After Ivy died, Eileen learned that Brigit's dream had been accurate, but the fifth child was not Eileen's.

§⟶⟵§

It had been nearly a month since Ivy's death before Eileen returned to the bed they once shared. She was still getting used to the quiet and the absence of warmth and bulk on the other side of the bed, but she could at last finally sleep there. Now it was time to go through Ivy's things. Paddy already had Ivy's fishing gear. The clothes and whatever else Eileen didn't want to keep would go to Goodwill or into the trash. The girls had offered to help, but she wanted this last intimate duty for herself. His clothing would raise ghosts of their life together, and there would be tears. But she was ready to do this now.

Eileen opened the door to Ivy's deep walk-in closet, a twin to her own next to it. She began with his collection of fifty-three ties, some of which were outdated. She smiled. He always had a hard time parting with ties. In fact, he'd stored a box of much older ties up on the shelf. A few of the ties she was now appraising were significant for her as well, so she put them aside as keepsakes. She found if she didn't look closely at the rest of his clothes and just quickly packed them, she could spare herself the pain of remembering when he last wore them.

The empty hangars looked so lonely, but there was a lifetime of odds and ends on the high shelf still to be gone through. Eileen fetched the step stool from the kitchen, climbed up, and removed boxes containing old shoes, belts, the ties that no one would wear today, and sports equipment and memorabilia. Maybe Paddy will want some of this memorabilia. She shook her head. Ivy, love, you were such a pack rat.

Then she spotted an old cardboard shoebox tucked away at the back of the shelf, almost out of her reach. That shoe company had gone out of business not long after the end of World War II. She scooted it to the front, took it down, and carried it to the paisley reading chair in the corner of the sunny bedroom. She sat with it in her lap and brushed the dust off the lid. The box chilled her. She shook herself. It's probably just stuff from when he was in the service. He rarely talked about the war and never shared any pictures or mementos from that time with her.

She thought about throwing it away without opening it. After all, it had to be stuff from before they were married, and if he'd wanted her to see whatever was in the box, he would have shared it with her. Eileen knew what had been in the other boxes because he'd told her about them with orders not to throw them out whenever a cleaning frenzy overtook her. This one he hadn't told her about, and he had hidden it, yes, hidden it way at the back of the shelf behind all the other boxes. Whatever was in the box was too important to him to throw away and something he wanted to hide from her.

Oh, I'm being silly. We had no secrets from each other! He was such a pack rat; he hardly ever threw anything away. Besides, there might be something in here that Paddy and the girls would want.

She lifted the black lid from the cream-colored box. On top were pictures of his ship and photos of smiling young sailors, none of whom she recognized, although their names were on the back. There was a picture of him with a few young men from other military branches coming out of a white clapboard church. On the back, he'd written "FDR's death, representative guard for local memorial service at St. Mary's in Carnegie." She was only in her late teens at the time, but she remembered the memorial service at her own church. She dug deeper and found playbills for the Pittsburgh Playhouse, a post card of the Fort Pitt Hotel, and finally a picture of Ivy in his uniform with a lovely, round-faced, blond woman. The back of the picture was labeled "Rayna and me at a USO dance, March 1945."

Eileen laughed. How sentimental. He'd kept a picture of a girlfriend from a time in his life long before he'd met her. Did he think she'd be jealous? How silly. He had made his life with her, created their near-perfect family with her, treated her like the lady of the manor. She never doubted his love for her.

She looked for more pictures only to find a single letter. The return address on the envelope read, "Rayna Migielski" along with a Carnegie address. Eileen read the letter and now understood why the box had so chilled her. Ivy did have a secret.

She dropped the letter to the floor. So cold, so hollow. That's how she felt. The letter mocked their entire life together. If only he had told her. Would it have made a difference to her? No, she loved him and still would have married him, but keeping this secret from her put the lie to their bond, which she had always believed was grounded in trust. She had to accept the reality before her: He thought her heart too small to accept this part of himself he'd left in the past.

Rayna wrote that they had a daughter, but that she want-ed nothing to do with him. Why? Ivy would have married her, and from the way he so cherished their children, he would have made a princess of that little girl.

Eileen gazed at the bed they had shared. She would not be sleeping in it tonight. She might never sleep in it again.

The coldness within her was so intense it burned. She picked up the letter and shoved it into the box. She wanted to crush it into particles of dust. Tears scorched her eyes. She stood, whimpered, and then raged. She trembled and snapped her head around the room. Instead of the familiar warmth she sought, she found a foreign land she was seeing for the first time. She strode to Ivy's closet and vaulted the box against the opposite wall inside before slamming the door. She dropped to the carpet and wailed.

It was like losing him all over again.

$\qquad$

Eileen closed the book in her lap. It took nearly eight months back then, but she had finally returned to their bed. The remembrances her children had of Ivy reassured her that, despite this one secret, their bond had been true. Her own memories of the depth of their life together added to this assurance. Ivy was the love of her life, and, together, they created a warm, loving home for their boisterous chil-dren. Ivy, an only child with no living relatives when they met, basked in the joy and hoi polloi of a large family—hers as well as their own.

When she recalled all that he had told her of his early life, she came to understand why he kept this incident from his past secret. At age ten, Ivy's mother had returned to Sweden and left him in the hands of an abusive father. A year after she left, her relatives sent word to his father that she had died, and they would welcome Ivy into their home if his father would send him. Young Ivy wept as his father celebrated his wife's death with drink. Later, the man beat the boy and warned him never to speak of his mother or her people. All Ivy had was her picture, which he kept well hidden. Eileen looked up at the mantle where that picture stood along with so many other family photographs.

Then, not long before the war broke out, Ivy became engaged to a girl from a neighboring farm. His father had fostered the match with the plan of uniting their properties. Despite his father's crass purpose, Ivy had grown to love the girl. The day of the wedding, however, Ivy stood at the altar alone. News came that the evening before, the girl had eloped with her cousin, who had fled Bavaria to make his life in the United States and escape a war that was sure to come. His father stormed at Ivy but did not strike him. Ivy had served the old man some of his own meat when he was seventeen, and his father feared a repeat of the beating. Ivy told Eileen he did not weep at the loss of his sweetheart, as deep as the loss felt. The girl had to know what his father was like. He couldn't blame her for not wanting to live in a house where she and their children might be harmed when Ivy was not there. And, for all the girl knew, Ivy might turn out to be like his father.

When Pearl Harbor shattered the peace of a country whose citizens felt removed from the rumblings of war in Europe and the Far East, Ivy enlisted in the Navy, as much to get away from his father as for any patriotic fervor. At the end of the war, Ivy returned home to a cancer-husked father. A year later, the old man died, and Ivy sold the farm to the family of his former sweetheart. Eileen remembered how he had smiled at the irony of it. He moved to Pittsburgh and went to work for an insurance company, the same insurance company, where a few years later, Eileen came to work.

Ivy had shared all of this with her, but insisted that it remain in the past. He did not want their children or her family to have their lives blotted with his early misery. He only wanted the joy for their children that he had found with her and her family. So Paddy and the girls and her family knew only that Ivy had been brought up on a farm in Beaver Falls and that both of his parents were dead.

What Ivy had left out of his history was Rayna and their child. After so many losses, he must have feared he might look as cold as his father and lose her and the joyful future they could create—did create.

She wondered why Rayna had been so angry. Was it the stigma of having an illegitimate child? Illegitimate children were not so unusual during wartime. Eileen recalled a lot of quick marriages and an unusual number of "premature" babies during and after the war. Could it be that she hadn't loved Ivy? Then why did she sleep with him? Ivy was a healthy man, but she knew he would only take up with a decent woman—and considering what he'd saved in the shoe box, he probably was in love with Rayna. She wondered what had happened to Ivy's little girl and thought about contacting Rayna, but Eileen found no Migielskis in the phone book. Perhaps Rayna had married, and Ivy's daughter had the family every child should have. Maybe Ivy was Rayna's secret. She decided that it might be best for everyone for the past to remain the past.

Eileen's life was full with family after Ivy died—grandchildren, the nieces and nephews, always something going on in the family, and poor, sad Jimmy who had needed them after Angie and the baby died. Although many suitors wanted her company, she believed no one could give her what she'd shared with Ivy, and family was more than enough for her.

But Jimmy? No, it wasn't the kind of life meant for Jimmy. There should be more for him than the leftovers of family shared with bachelor uncles. Jimmy needed a mate, and it wasn't too late for children. Eileen yawned and snapped her book shut.

Please, God, no more disappointments for our Jimmy!

❦TWENTY–SIX❦

AFTER NEARLY TWO weeks watching the station, Marco Cantuso was gratified to see that Shannon and Santello often came and went together.

Today's the day, Tony. I'm sending those two cops to Hell!

He wiped the sweat from his tanned, narrow face and removed the Smith and Wesson .38 Special from the glove compartment, another of Tony's possessions he'd inherited. He'd cleaned and oiled it the way Tony showed him. He laid the loaded weapon on the seat. He was ready. He'd sit there all day if he had to. Hell, he'd come back tomorrow, and the day after, and the day after that until the two showed up together. He could go on parking in different spots or hanging out on the sidewalk until the perfect moment.

He glanced down at the litter of food wrappings, bags, soda cups, and beer bottles on the floor. Tony wouldn't like that.

I'll clean it out when this is over, Tony. The Judge will be as good as new. I promise.

A Crown Vic pulled into a space in front of the station halfway down the block from Marco's Ford Galaxy. He started the engine in case it was them. All his windows were already down, and he'd smeared mud on the license plates. He figured if he shot the driver, the other one would run to the fallen officer. Then he could shoot that one, too. He'd gone over his plan again and again, even practicing the drive by. It was perfect but he had to be fast.

It was that Detective Shannon who got out of the driver's side, head thrown back, laughing at something his partner said. Marco grabbed the gun and floored the Galaxy into the nearly empty street. The detectives turned to look at the speeding car.

Yeah, look, you shitheads! Last thing you'll see is The Judge.

Marco slowed and shot the man twice as he passed him. He tapped the brake as the man crumpled to the ground.

One down.

He rolled into the other lane a couple car lengths ahead of them and angled The Judge for a clear view. He braked and aimed at the woman when she whipped around the Crown Vic to the fallen detective, gun drawn. She got off a round before he could fire.

Marco felt searing heat in his chest and saw his blood spurting out with each heartbeat. He fired, but the shot went wild, hitting the windshield of the Crown Vic. God, his chest hurt, and there was so much blood covering him!

Wasn't supposed to be like this!

Everything dimmed. He shook his head. Refocusing, he saw her check the downed detective and rise up to take a firing stance. Policemen with drawn guns poured out of the station.

"Throw out your gun and get out of the car with your hands up!"

Fighting off the gray fog, he trained his sights on the woman and fired.

Missed again! Damn! Wasn't supposed to go like this. Tony! Tony, help me!

The last thing he saw were a handful of police officers and the woman firing at him.

❧TWENTY-SEVEN❧

CAPTAIN MCILHENY LEFT Mercy Hospital after learning it would be some time before Shannon was out of surgery. Santello promised to call him as soon as she knew anything. She scanned the hospital waiting room. It barely held all of Shannon's family members and close friends, but few had left, even though many of them had been standing so the elderly and frail could sit for a couple of hours. Santello knew many of them from Shannon's birthday parties, as well as from Shannon's wedding and Angie's funeral. She had talked to Shannon's nieces earlier and told them to go to Eileen's and prepare a meal for her. She would need them to fill a near-empty house with their comfort.

In one corner, Eileen's cousin Brigit sat mumbling, her small, pale face wet with tears below pixie bangs of dark hair. "I didn't see this coming. I would have warned him, but I didn't see this coming."

Santello recognize Angie's mother, a stooped, gray-haired woman, whose face was lined like a road map. She was leading a small group of women in the rosary. Santello shook her head, smiling sadly.

Just like my family.

She spotted Eileen, face drawn, eyes red and swollen, staring at her—or rather, at her jacket. Paddy, his arm around her, followed his mother's gaze. His mouth dropped open. Santello glanced down at the brown splotches of Shannon's blood on her tan jacket. Eileen must have been too distraught to notice them earlier. Santello had hopped into the ambulance with the unconscious Shannon without any thought of the condition of her clothes. She was going to stick with her partner all the way. Her old partner had done the same for her.

She wove through the milling Shannons, McIntyres, O'Donnells, O'Reillys, Bugielskis, Pellegrinos, and the others to Eileen and her son. "Paddy, you planning to catch flies with that mouth?"

He promptly closed it and looked away.

Santello hugged Eileen. "He's going to pull through, Ei. Doc Bugielski won't let his cousin die on the operating table. He took care of me when I was shot, and I'm good as new. Hey, Doc's older now, more experienced. Jimmy will be fine."

Eileen dabbed her pink nose with a crumpled tissue, nodding her head. "Oh, I know something like this can happen any time to a policeman. It's just that you never think it will be one of your own."

"Yeah, you never know."

"I'm so glad you stayed with him."

"He's my partner."

"Partner." Eileen's eyes widened. "Rose, he was supposed to have dinner with someone tonight, but I don't know how to get hold of her."

"Uncle Jimmy's seeing someone?"

"Hush, Paddy!" Eileen looked around to see if anyone had heard them.

"Oh, that's right! Uh, don't worry. I'll take care of it." Looking around, Santello said, "Gotta find a phone."

Eileen lowered her voice to a whisper. "You mean you know her?"

"Uh, yeah, but Shannon told me if I spilled the beans to you, he'd transfer to another division.

"Is she on the force?"

"Sorry."

"No. If she was, she'd know about Jimmy getting shot." Eileen shook her head, smiling. "Oh, go. Just go and make that call. I hope she doesn't give up on him after this."

"Me, too."

As Santello turned away, she caught the grin on Paddy's face. "Uncle Jimmy's seeing someone?"

I have a feeling that's one secret that won't be a secret for long.

Santello found a bank of pay phones at the end of the secluded corridor. She found Liz's phone number in her notebook, plunked coins into the phone, and dialed. The phone barely rang twice before Liz answered.

"Hello? Jim?"

"Uh, no. It's Rose . . . Rose Santello. I'm just calling to tell you that . . . well, Jimmy can't make it tonight."

"What do you mean he can't make it tonight? And isn't he capable of cancelling his own dates?"

"I'm sorry, Ms. Michaels. The reason I'm making the call is because Jimmy's in surgery."

"He's what! What happened? Is he going to be okay?"

"Please, calm down. He's got the best surgeon in Pittsburgh. He's going to be fine.

If I say that enough times, maybe it will come true.

"Detective Santello, please tell me what happened."

"Please, just Rose. . . . Last year we put away a guy, and he got killed in prison. Guy had a kid brother who came after us because we arrested him. When we were getting out of the car in front of the precinct this afternoon, the kid pulled up beside us and shot Jimmy. When I ran around the car to get to Jimmy, the kid shot at us again. Our officers came running out of the station when they heard the commotion, and we killed the shooter. The ambulance came in minutes, and here we are at Mercy Hospital."

There was silence on the other end of the line.

"Liz? I mean, Ms. Michaels, are you there?"

"Sorry. Yes, I'm here. . . . He didn't have a chance, did he? He didn't even know he'd been shot. Is he really going to be all right?"

"We're all praying. But yeah. I'm sure Jimmy's going to be fine. Doc Bugielski pulled me through. He's not going to do less for his cousin."

Please, God, make it true.

"What can I do?"

"Well, I guess you can pray. And maybe tomorrow, or when he's up to it, you can visit him. But call ahead to make sure all of his relatives aren't camped out here."

"Why should that make a difference?"

"It's a long story."

"Rose, please call me as soon as he's out of surgery."

"I will."

"No matter how late it is."

"Okay."

About an hour after Santello returned to the waiting room, which looked even more crowded than when she left, tall, thin, gray-blond Dr. Boleslaw Bugielski, known to family and friends as Bolek, sauntered into the waiting room. Everyone fell silent and gave their full attention to the surgeon. He scanned the room until he saw Eileen. He crossed to her and took her hands. His serious hazel eyes made large by black-framed glasses brightened with his slow smile. "He beat the guy with the scythe, Ei. He's going to be fine."

The roar from the waiting room could be heard out on the street. A few yelled out "Way to go, Bolek!" Tears spilled down Eileen's face as she thanked him.

"It could have been worse. He could have been gut shot—that's a painful, ugly recovery. Right, Rose?"

"Yeah. I had days I thought about eating my gun."

"The bullets were higher but missed his heart and barely nicked a lung. It was quite a mess, and he's lost a lot of blood, but he'll recover fully."

"Bolek, why'd he lose consciousness when he was shot? I was gut shot and never lost consciousness—even made an arrest," Santello said.

"Who knows, Rose? Everybody's different." He glanced around the waiting room. "Go home, everybody, and get some sleep. You too, Ei. Jimmy can have visitors tomorrow." He chuckled as the crowd began dwindling. "But not all of you at once."

"Don't worry, Bolek. I'll set up a schedule," his wife said. She waved at Eileen on her way out. "I'll be in touch, Eileen."

Santello said she could pray. Liz didn't consider herself a religious person, despite the visits from her mother and grandmother. It wasn't that she didn't believe there was more than this life—after all, she had proof. However, when she thought about her own losses, she was sometimes—though not without a twinge of guilt because of all she did have—angry at the Creator.

She had prayed to become part of her father's family, but she found rejection instead. She had prayed for a baby, but lost it. Was it asking too much to want her own baby and her own family? She didn't think He was a vengeful God, and it made no sense to her that a loving God would punish creatures as fragile and flawed as human beings. After all, hadn't He made them this way?

Liz saw existence as a boot camp for humans, who were driven by hormones, fear, addictions, and need. She just couldn't understand why He didn't do more to assuage the anguish of being human. What good was suffering?

A number of manuscripts about Gnostic Christianity and New Age beliefs had crossed her desk. She found them intriguing. Many of these books proposed that you set up your own challenges before you were born. That would certainly take the onus off the Creator but raise a question about the value of prayer. However, none of the writers said that prayer was useless. In fact, some said prayer to the Divine could help to reduce the severity of a bad experience, unless it was one you had specifically charted to be extreme because you wanted to learn a particular lesson. In that case, there was no wiggle room. Thing was, there was no way to tell which experiences had wiggle room.

So on the chance it would help, she would pray. Liz was just getting to know Jim Shannon, and she wanted to get to know him better. In the few times they had talked, especially the time at her dinner table and the hour-long phone call he made to confirm their date, she discovered him to be a gentle, compassionate man with a sense of humor. He made her laugh, and she found it so easy to talk to him. She was comfortable with him. He wasn't hard on the eyes, either.

Please, God. Let him live. She hesitated. I'd like to get to know him better. She instantly regretted her selfishness. Oh, let him live a long and happy life, even if I don't get to know him better. Please, God?

✤✤✤

Liz floated in a kayak on the still surface of an aquamarine sea. Sunlight beamed through the very depths, revealing emerald-hued white sand, pink coral, sea cucumbers, brilliantly-colored plants and a school of hurtling dolphins that occasionally breached the surface ahead of her in joyful abandon.

Suddenly, her kayak rocked. The waters became rough, waves growing higher and higher, sometimes breaking over her. Looking down, she found her hands dry but empty of any paddle. Had she ever had a paddle? Panic seized her. She searched around for land or any other means of rescue from the surging waters. No land, but off to the side, she spotted a large boat. It was so large, it had to be a cruise ship—or maybe a Coast Guard cutter, possibly an outrageously large yacht. She yelled and waved her arms.

Liz suddenly felt herself speeding forward and, fearful of falling out, grasped the sides of the kayak. Several dolphins surrounded her tiny craft, two at a time taking turns shoving the kayak forward. As she neared the yacht, people saw her and waved. She heard a musical trumpet sound, not a horn blast, and the boat started toward her. The boat—she could see it was a yacht, now—slowed as it closed in on her. An older, slender, blond man wearing a captain's hat threw her a life preserver. She found herself on the deck, completely dry, wearing a gauzy white sundress, without any memory of having been hauled up over the side or drying off and changing clothes.

She was amazed at the size of the yacht, but was more astounded at the huge number of passengers. They were all smiling, talking, drinking, eating, dancing—and she recognized some of them. Her smiling mother and grandmother were talking to the man who rescued her. Her mouth dropped open—he was her father.

Looking very much alive, they strolled over to her, and turned her around to look at all the other people. Her mother hugged her and said, "They're all family, Lizzy."

Liz saw Jim Shannon with a tiny, blond toddler clinging to his neck. His head was thrown back in laughter at something the young man at his side had said. They resembled each other, and, as the young man turned toward her, she saw he was Paddy.

Liz heard ringing as she thought to herself, "Oh, no! Are they relat—?"

"Are they—" Liz mumbled as she opened her eyes and reached for the phone. She blinked and rubbed her eyes, feeling uneasy. "Hello?"

"Ms. Michaels? Rose. He's out of surgery, and everything's good."

"Oh, that's great news!"

"Yeah, it sure is. Last thing I wanted to do was to have to break in a new partner."

Liz was silent.

"I'm joking. Cop humor."

"Oh."

"If you plan to see a lot of Jimmy, you better get used to stuff like that. It helps us get through a lot of crap."

"Okay."

"Gotta go. Doc's dropping me off at the station."

"Oh, and, Rose . . . it's Liz."

After hanging up, Liz realized she'd fallen asleep in the chair waiting for Rose to call back. She had a dream but she couldn't remember all of it—only flashes of dolphins and the sound of a trumpet. Something about it, though, made her very uncomfortable. Maybe it would come to her later.

༄✿TWENTY–EIGHT✿༄

THE CORRIDOR EMITTED vague scents of vanilla, disinfectant cleaners, and rubbing alcohol. Either someone had just baked cookies or her grandmother was here. Liz saw Santello in Shannon's flower- and balloon-bedecked hospital room, deep in what looked like serious conversation. When she was almost to the door, she paused, set down the heavy food hamper she'd brought, and moved out of sight to listen.

"Look, Jimmy, we've been partners a long time, and I don't want to have to train a new one. As it is, your substitute is getting on my nerves, even if he is my Aunt Anita's cousin."

Shannon looked at her through drooping eyes. "I'm tired, Rose. I don't want to talk about it anymore."

"No way, Seamus Aloysius! We're going to settle this right now."

"Look, I can't remember being shot. Last thing I remember is laughing at one of your jokes and then waking up in this room. Leave me alone."

Her face reddened. "You can't quit, Jimmy!"

Shannon winced as he clutched the bed rail, his eyes wide. "Watch me. I did two tours in Nam as an MP without so much as a scratch. And look at how many years we've partnered without an incident. Even when I was a beat cop, no one shot at me."

Santello huffed and crossed her arms.

"Maybe if I'd seen it coming, could have defended myself, even could remember it, I'd feel different." He shook his head. "But this . . . I feel like my luck ran out. It feels too final, Rose. Like I could've been gone and never come out of it. This was the deal breaker."

She opened her mouth, but Shannon didn't give her a chance to counter.

"The crap never ends. I'm tired of running down wife-killers and seeing them get nothing but a slap on the wrist. How many times have we run the same perp through the courts? Huh? And the babies and kids, starved or beaten to death by hopped up mothers and boyfriends? We don't even make a tiny scratch let alone a dent in all the crime, and it's not getting any better. I don't think it's worth my life."

"Can't you see how much worse it would be without us?"

Shannon shook his head and lay back on the pillow.

Liz decided it was time to put in an appearance. She smiled and walked in lugging the food hamper. "Hi, since we missed out on dinner Friday night, I've brought us lunch. Of course, it doesn't compare to hospital food." She glanced at Rose. "There's enough for all three of us."

They stared, the heat between them slowly ebbing away as they found smiles for her. Rose vacated the chair next to his bed. "Here, Liz, have a seat. Would love to try whatever you brought, but I've got to get back to the station. We'll talk later, Jimmy."

He nodded, and Rose strode from the room.

Liz spotted the spirits of her mother and grandmother on the other side of Jimmy's bed.

What are they up to?

"Well, I see they still have you hooked up to an IV. Does that mean you're not eating?"

"No. It's just for antibiotics and pain meds. It's supposed to come out today. I've been wondering if the stuff's been messing up my sense of smell. I've been smelling vanilla all morning."

"Oh?" She glanced at the two spirits. They smiled at her and then faded.

Shannon grinned at her and sat up straighter, which made him wince. He depressed a button to raise the head of his bed. "So, what did you bring me?"

"What? Oh." Liz pulled a serious face. "Peach-flavored cream of wheat, a banana health shake, and a thermos of chamomile tea. I figured it was too soon for regular food."

His face wilted. "I did have what passed for pancakes and eggs for breakfast."

She grinned.

"Okay, is that any way to treat an injured man? Come on. What do you have there?"

Liz pushed the rolling tray table to his bedside and began unpacking. "This is a thermos of my grandmother's chicken soup—"

"Ew, how old is it?"

She stared at him as though his attempt at middle school humor did not in any way impress her.

Shannon smiled.

"And I brought the fixings for sandwiches—fresh-baked pumpernickel bread from Steinmetz, roast beef from my own kitchen, Gerald Kernan's homegrown romaine lettuce and beefsteak tomatoes, some imported Irish butter, horseradish and a variety of mustards as well as some mayo. There's also a container of pickles I put up myself last fall." The last item she removed with a flourish. "And for dessert—I baked you my luscious lemon meringue pie." Removing another thermos, she said, "Oh, and I also brought my special coffee."

Shannon beamed like a kid who had gotten a BMX bike for his birthday. After he had some of the soup, Liz put together half a sandwich according to his specifications and watched him enjoy every bite.

"Ready for more?"

"After that half, I'm afraid I might not be able to keep more down."

"Are you okay? Should I get the nurse?"

"I'm fine. I just don't want to push it. I'd really be embarrassed to get sick and lose all that great food in front of you."

"Could you manage a slice of pie?"

"Hm. Why don't you have a slice, and I'll just take a bite?"

"You know, I'm not a dessert person." Her eyes twinkled. "It will be hard, but just for you, I'll force myself."

When they finished, Liz repacked the basket. "I'm going to leave all of this with you in case you get hungry later. If not, you can share it with your family and friends—or the nurses. . . . So what were you and Rose talking about when I came in? You both looked upset."

He lost his smile. "I'm thinking of getting into another line of work."

"Oh, what would you do?"

"I have a degree in criminal justice. With my experience, I could join a PI agency or even open one of my own. Or, I could get a law degree and become a prosecutor." He paused a moment. "Of course, they sometimes get shot at, too, and I'd still be dealing with the same injustice issues. I really don't have to work for a living, but I'm too young to just lie around, doing nothing."

"I didn't know policemen made so much money."

"They don't. Are you familiar with Shannon Trucking?"

"I've seen the trucks. Now, don't tell me you own the company."

"Along with my four sisters. Our parents started that company, and now that they're gone, each of us has an interest in it. In fact, one of my sisters is the President and another is Vice President of Operations."

"How nice for you."

"We each have a modest trust fund, too."

"Thoughtful parents. . . . So Rose doesn't like the idea of you leaving the job?"

"She thinks she'll miss me. If I had my own agency, I'd hire her in a heartbeat. For that matter, she could leave and join an agency, too. She has enough time in, she could retire tomorrow."

"Why doesn't she want to do that?"

"She says she enjoys going after the bad guys, and sneaking around taking pictures of cheating husbands just doesn't do it for her."

"Well, I learned sometime ago that no one else can make your choices for you. Besides, unwanted advice falls on deaf ears." Liz smiled at him, and he returned her smile. His eyes told her he was grateful she was giving him his space.

§↗↖↘

Eileen stepped out of the elevator and glanced toward Shannon's room. A striking, well-dressed blond woman in the room looked like she was getting ready to leave. There was something familiar about her. As Eileen approached the room, she saw the woman laugh. The space between her teeth was like Paddy's. Eileen caught her breath. The woman could have been a softer, pretty version of her dead husband. Did Jimmy see the resemblance?

The woman slipped out of the room, looked back at Shannon a moment, waved, and then continued toward Eileen and the elevators. Eileen regained her composure and returned her smile as they passed each other. She couldn't help marveling at the extraordinary blue of the woman's eyes. Yes, other than the eyes, she could be Ivy's daughter.

Strolling into Shannon's room, Eileen smiled. "Was that pretty lady in the Chanel suit who just walked out of here the Mystery Woman?"

Shannon regarded his sister with a cat-that-ate-the-canary smile, but said nothing.

"Okay, be that way."

"Sorry, Ei. . . . Hey, she left some really great food, but I couldn't eat all of it. It's there in that hamper. Have some. As a matter of fact, I think I could get down another half sandwich. Anyway, if I barf, it won't be anything you haven't seen before."

"Eat slowly and chew thoroughly, and you shouldn't have a problem. Although if you do get sick, it won't be me cleaning up after you. There are orderlies to take care of such things."

She made Shannon and herself sandwiches while she planned how she would get the real dope about the woman out of Rose. It was more than just curiosity now. She wanted to know if this woman could be who she thought she was. She turned to her brother with an innocent smile and handed him his sandwich. "By the way, Paddy will come by later tonight."

"He didn't come home from the dorm?"

"No, too much going on at school. You know, without you there, the place is pretty empty."

Eileen immediately regretted what she'd said. She saw that look in his eyes when he thought she was lonely and unhappy. She hoped he wasn't going to suggest she go out with one of the men who still called her.

"Why don't you take Rose out to dinner tonight? It'll give you some company. Besides, she's pretty mad at me about leaving the force. Maybe you could put out the fire. Talk some sense into her." He put on his most charming grin. "If anyone can get through to her, it's my big sister Eileen." He filled his mouth with sandwich, and tomato juice and mustard dribbled down his chin.

"Cute, Jimmy."

Eileen grabbed a napkin and wiped his chin before he could do it for himself and realized he was playing the sympathy card with his look-at-me-Sis-I-really-need-your-help act. The routine had worked on her since he was old enough to figure out how to manipulate them all. She guessed it always would.

"Even though I'd just as soon see you doing something less dangerous, didn't I tell you to wait awhile before making that decision? You're still in shock and depressed. A serious trauma to the body can have that effect, you know—not to mention whatever drugs they're pumping into you. You might feel differently in a few weeks."

Shannon shrugged liked he did when he was a kid and didn't want to argue with her. He grimaced at the pain.

"You could have at least waited to tell her after you got out of the hospital."

Shannon shook his head. "I don't know, Ei. You and I have talked a lot about how the job drains me. Well, getting shot did it for me. I don't think I'm going to feel any different in a few weeks. It would really take something pretty drastic to change my mind."

The circles under his eyes and the way the hospital bed and tubes and wires attached to him made him look so vulnerable caught at her. He really didn't need to play the sympathy card with the condition he was in now.

"Okay, Jimmy, I'll talk to Rose. I'll take her to Angelino's. I know she likes the food there."

She bit into the savory sandwich and smiled to herself. *And I'll wheedle the information on this mystery woman out of her, too.* She glanced at Shannon and chewed contentedly. *Bet you didn't think of that, little brother.*

ᘒᜩᜩᜩᘓ

Angelino's was the stereotypical Italian restaurant with candle-stuffed Chianti bottles, red-checked tablecloths, and food made from scratch by three generations of Italians. On the weekends, the dimly-lit restaurant attracted diners from as far away as Weirton, West Virginia, and Steubenville, Ohio. Tonight, Rose and Eileen found it less crowded than usual. They savored their eggplant parmesan and veal Marsala entrees with wine and sipped coffee that tasted like it might have been brewed in Rome. Reflections of the candle flame swayed in the cups on their table.

"I'm glad you could have dinner with me, Rose. But dinner doesn't seem like much of a thank you for looking out for Jimmy."

"No thanks needed, Ei. We're partners. He'd have done the same for me."

"I know you're not happy about Jimmy's decision to quit the force."

"You kidding? I'm downright furious!" She slapped the table, jostling the candle and cups. "Jimmy's a damned good cop. . . . Maybe if you talked to him?"

Eileen shook her head. "Rose, I've always worried about him on the job, and his getting shot hit us both with just how dangerous the job is."

Santello nodded, then looked up at Eileen with peppercorn eyes as intense as the spice. "Every one of us cops knows the dangers. That's why we're trained to take precautions. We don't dwell on if today is the day we buy it. We just use our training to reduce the chances."

"Training didn't do a thing for him when that boy shot him. Jimmy lost so much blood, he almost died."

"Eileen, that was a fluke. No one could have predicted any of us getting shot in front of the station. It was as far out there as getting hit by a drunken cabbie." She smirked. "More likely to get hit by a drunken cabbie. . . . He needs to take some time to think about this. He's too good at the job. He really makes a difference whether he thinks so or not." Santello raised her hand like she was swearing an oath. "And I promise to take better care of your brother in the future."

Eileen smiled and nodded. "I don't know. Jimmy has been unhappy with the job for a long time. He never shares the details of his cases, but some nights he comes home, and his eyes look like they've seen more than he can stomach."

"I think that started after Angie and the baby died. It colored everything for him. And other than a little fishing, I don't think he's been on a real vacation since then. Please. Talk to him."

Eileen put her cup down and sat back in her chair. "I did tell him to give it some time before making a decision, but as my three sisters and I learned early on, no matter how we tortured him, once Jimmy made up his mind, that was it. . . . Maybe both of you should leave. Start your own PI agency?"

"You know that's not my style, Ei."

Eileen nodded. "I'll talk to him again. However, if he leaves, I know you'll still be friends."

"Yeah. Goes without saying." Santello smiled slyly. "Of course, he may not have a lot of time for friends in the near future."

Eileen squinted at Rose and then got it. "Or family. The Mystery Woman, right? You know, I saw her leaving when I visited Jimmy today."

"Oh, yeah?"

"She's very attractive in an icy way."

"Funny you should say that because I used to call her the Ice Queen."

"Oh, really? Why?"

"Well, you saw her. She's so . . . so perfect. She doesn't blather like a lot of women either."

"Uh-huh. How did Jimmy meet her?"

"Ei!"

"Look, we're going to find out sooner or later. I'll keep what you tell me to myself and let Jimmy tell us all about her when he's ready. Oh, and you do want me to ask Jimmy to think a little more about it before finalizing his decision to leave the force, don't you?"

Santello threw her hands up. "Okay, but you didn't hear it from me. Did Jimmy tell you about our investigation into the guy who fell from The Lafayette?"

"Jimmy doesn't talk about his cases with us, but I do re member hearing something about it on the news. I don't recall the details. Maybe there weren't any."

"Well, the guy was her ex-husband, and he fell five stories from her terrace."

Eileen paled. "Did she have anything to do with it?"

"Naw. I was pretty sure at first she did, but it turns out the guy had a heart attack and fell. She wasn't there."

Eileen breathed easier. "Oh."

"Yeah, we still can't figure out why he was in her place. Got in with a lock pick."

"So who is she?"

"Liz Michaels. She's part owner of a publishing company, Kernan, Feinstein and Company."

"Really." Tumblers clicked in Eileen's head—the place where Paddy worked, and Liz Michaels was his mentor. Had he mentioned her to Jimmy?

"Yeah. I didn't like her at first, but I found out she wasn't born rich and worked her way up. Jimmy thinks she looks a little like Mona, but I don't see it. The bum she was married to made her life hell."

"Why would a smart woman like that marry a bum?"

"He was from some high-class family in Ohio. Guess he wasn't such a loser when she married him."

Eileen looked down at her plate. "Her parents must've been there for her."

"The mother died when she was nineteen. Birth certificate didn't list the father's name. Think there was a step-father, but looks like he vanished some time ago. She changed her name, too."

"Who? The mother?"

"No, Liz. Changed it from Migielski to Michaels when she graduated from Pitt."

"Wonder why?"

"Probably for business. People don't seem to like dealing with people who have ethnic names, especially Slavish or Italian names. You know the stereotypes all of us get plas-tered with."

"Yes, like all Poles are really dumb—Poles like Bolek Bu-gielski." They both snickered.

"She didn't take Payne's name when they married. Makes sense. Less of a hassle not having to change all your records."

Eileen thought a moment. "Or maybe she wanted to keep an identity she had come to value." Or one that would make it harder for her to be found by her father if her name hit the papers.

☙TWENTY-NINE☙

EILEEN SAT IN Ivy's recliner and stared at the photo of her dead husband and Rayna. They were both fair, but there was no doubt which of them Liz resembled, although she must have gotten her eyes from her mother. She replaced the photo in Ivy's shoebox of mementos—she had no idea why she'd kept it—and leaned back in the chair. So that lovely, talented woman who's caught Jimmy's eye is Ivy's daughter.

Now free of the rage that had nearly incinerated her heart when she first discovered Ivy's secret, she smiled. Ivy would have been so proud of her, just as he was of their four. Of course, Ivy might have known about her success. Did he keep track of her, contact her? Only Liz could tell her that now.

I wonder if I'll have the opportunity once Jimmy learns of Liz's connection to the family. He might not be able to get past the shock of discovering that he's attracted to his step-

niece. If he does decide he can't go on seeing her, Eileen could simply let the past be with no one else the wiser. When she first learned about Ivy's secret, she'd decided leaving the past in the past might be better for everyone. That might still be the case for her family. After all, Liz, a successful woman, certainly had no need of her father's family.

Eileen glanced at the picture of Jimmy and Angie on the mantle. But Jimmy needed someone, deserved to love again. And Liz, despite her achievements and considering her failed marriage, might welcome a man like her brother into her life. Jimmy had learned respect and gentleness from a mother and four sisters. Eileen nodded. He was a good catch.

Still, how would her children respond? Her three girls and Paddy adored their father and might resent Liz for bringing to light a part of his past they would have trouble understanding. Eileen might be able to repair some of the damage by sharing what their father's early life was like. They were adults and would surely understand how fear played a role in Ivy keeping his daughter secret, although it would help to understand why Rayna refused to have anything to do with him.

Paddy might wonder how much being her brother influenced his being awarded an internship. He'd need assurance that he'd come by the honor honestly. If Liz knew who her biological father was, she had to know Paddy was her half-brother.

Perhaps Rayna never told her who her father was. If Rayna was too angry to have anything to do with Ivy, she may have decided to close the book on it for Liz as well; and Paddy, as well as the family and "Uncle" Jimmy, would be as much of a surprise to her as she would be to them. Eileen closed her eyes. Life certainly was stranger than fiction.

Jimmy. There was no way she could keep this from him. He had a right to know before he got in too deep. Will he tell her she's part of the family? He might feel compelled to, regardless of whether or not he continues to see her. Family was important to all of the Shannons, and he would insist she meet her father's family and become as much part of it as she wanted.

And how do I feel about that? She does look so much like Ivy. It might be nice to have a living reminder of him around. Our four have some of his quirks, and Paddy, poor kid, got Ivy's teeth, but other than that, they all look like Shannons.

Eileen looked at the picture of Jimmy and Angie again. If Jimmy is attracted to her, she must be a decent human being. Now, how to break the news to him? He would be coming home from the hospital soon, so she'd wait until then. She glanced down at the box in her lap. Maybe she should just give him the box and go from there.

Eileen slipped out of the recliner with the box and turned out the light. I wonder how much sleep I'll get tonight. I can't help wondering how Liz will react if Jimmy tells her. Everyone, including Liz, will need time to recover from the shock.

§⁊⁊⥎⥦

"You know, Ei, I could have come to the table."

"It's your first day home from the hospital, Jimmy. Enjoy the coddling while it lasts."

She picked up their trays and headed to the kitchen. Shannon relaxed back into the recliner. "Besides, there's something we need to talk about, and I want you to be comfortable."

"I'm still quitting the force, so don't waste your breath," he yelled after her.

Eileen rolled her eyes. "I know, I know."

She returned with Ivy's shoe box, placed it on Shannon's lap, and sat on the edge of the armchair across from him.

"What's this?" He studied the box. One corner was split and taped. "This is a pretty old box."

"Open it."

Shannon lifted the lid and sifted through the military keepsakes. He found the picture of Ivy and Rayna and glanced up at Eileen. "Ivy's stuff?"

She nodded.

"So why are you showing me this?" He held up the photo. "Is it because of the woman in the photo?"

Eileen nodded again.

"Ei, you and Ivy met a long time after he got out of the service. He adored you. Isn't it a little late to get jealous over some woman from his past?"

"There's a letter in there. Read it."

He eyed her. "You're being awfully mysterious, Ei."

"Sorry, Jimmy. I wasn't sure about the best way to tell you."

"Tell me what?"

"Please, read the letter."

Finding the yellowed envelope, he removed the letter and began reading. When he finished, he studied Eileen a moment. "So our Ivy wasn't perfect."

She nodded and stared down at her hands. She'd never thought Ivy was perfect, just perfect for her.

"You know, though, that he loved you with everything he had in him."

She looked up. "I never doubted it."

Shannon looked back at the letter. "Hm, this Rayna sounds very angry. She doesn't explain why she doesn't want to have anything to do with him. Any idea if Ivy ever got to see his daughter?"

Eileen shrugged. "I found that box after Ivy died. I decided to contact this woman, but I couldn't find her in the phone book. After I thought about it, I decided to let it go. I figured she had married, and the daughter might be married with her own family. So I just let it go."

"Why are you revisiting it, now?"

She sat forward and took a deep breath. "I saw a woman who looked so much like Ivy that she just had to be his daughter. Look at the name in the return address on the envelope."

"Rayna Migielski." Shannon looked at his sister, his eyes blinking as his brain got busy connecting details from Santello's research.

"Her daughter is Elizabeth Rayna Migielski. You know her as Liz Michaels."

Shannon, open-mouthed and wide-eyed, dropped the envelope. "My God! She's my niece?"

"Step-niece." Maybe this wasn't the best way to tell him after all.

Shannon shook his head, then looked up at the pictures on the mantle. He ran his hand through his hair and looked back at her like he did at age six when he'd awakened from a nightmare. He always ran to his big sister when he was scared.

"Don't panic, Jimmy. She's no blood relation. There's no need to stop seeing her."

He rubbed his temples. "I don't know Ei. This could get very complicated. And she might not be able to get past our connection. Oh God, how is all this going to work with the rest of the family? Argh! Why does life have to be so difficult?" Suddenly he frowned and squinted at Eileen. "How did you put all this together?"

"You know, Jimmy, for all the time you spent with Ivy, I can't understand why you didn't see the resemblance. I saw it immediately."

Shannon shook his head. "I did, but what reason would I have to think she might be Ivy's daughter? I thought maybe she had some Swedish ancestry. . . . But how did you learn her name? Wait . . . Rose!"

Eileen grinned.

"Yeah, Rose did the background check on her. When Mrs. Payne mentioned that Liz had changed her name, I asked Rose about it. It didn't seem important. Does Rose know who she is?"

"No. You and I are the only ones who know she's Ivy's daughter."

"Did you always know Ivy had a daughter?"

"I found that box after he died."

"Ei, are you okay?"

It is what it is. I've had a lot more time than you with Ivy's secret. Oh, I was furious at him for keeping this from me, but after I thought about all he'd gone through when he was young, I came to understand why he was afraid to tell me. I don't think he could have stood one more loss."

"What do you mean all he'd gone through?"

Eileen shared the details of Ivy's abandonment by his mother, her death, his father's physical abuse, and the broken engagement.

"It's hard to believe. He always seemed so lighthearted and full of pranks."

"Ivy didn't want any of the darkness from his past to affect us or the children. You know, when people know things like that about you, it colors how they see you. He didn't want pity. He didn't want people tiptoeing around him. He didn't want his children or anyone else wondering when he might turn into his father."

"Ivy was too decent to turn into that. He was a great father and fun to be around. He was such a happy guy."

Eileen smiled at the memory of her husband's antics with their children. Then she considered her brother. "And that's why I don't think you should shut the door on this relationship. This is the happiest I've seen you since . . . well, for a long time. Now, we need to talk to Paddy."

"Yeah. He's young, and he worshipped Ivy. I can see how this could be a real shock to him."

Eileen cocked her head. "You don't know, do you?"

"Know what? Cripes, Ei, what more is there?"

"She's Paddy's mentor at the publishing company."

Shannon shook his head and rolled his eyes. "He's an intern at Kernan, Feinstein and Company? I guess I wasn't paying very close attention when he talked about hoping he'd get that internship. This can't be real."

"Oh, it's very real."

"Think of the odds."

"Jimmy, remember Helen Misiak from church?"

"Yeah. She finally found her father when she was in her forties, right?"

"Uh-huh. And she learned that they'd lived in the same community at the same time in two different states. They probably passed each other in the stores."

"Really? Hm, I wonder if Liz knows who Paddy is."

"Depends. If her mother told her who her father was, then she knows. But unless Paddy specifically mentioned you, she probably doesn't know you're his uncle."

Shannon dropped his head into his hands. After a moment, he looked up. "You don't think Paddy got his internship because he's her brother, do you?"

"Jimmy, you know Paddy's very talented and bright. There's no question he got the position on his own merits. Anyway, it was one of the other executives who chose him. Besides, Liz might not know they're related. However, we need to talk to him before we do anything else. If she does know, she might tell him or let it slip. He'll have doubts, and he'll have quite a lot to digest as it is."

"What about the girls?"

"Before we involve the girls, we should probably talk to Liz to see how she feels. Then we'll know what to tell them and the rest of the family."

Shannon stared at his sister. "Oh God, the rest of the family!"

ᏋᏌᎬᎥTHIRTYᏋᏌᏋ

PADDY, SPEECHLESS AND white-faced, tossed the letter into the box and pushed it aside. He stared at Eileen and Shannon across the kitchen table like he had just learned his father was dead—again.

"Paddy, we know this is hard for you."

"Mom, hard for me? I thought he was perfect! I still miss him." He gestured at the box. "What am I supposed to do with this?"

Shannon cleared his throat. "Romances and illegitimate babies were pretty common during World War II. In fact, they're common in every war. It's the not knowing if the men are going to survive. People get careless."

Paddy reddened. "Don't you think I know that, Uncle Jim? I'm not thirteen any more. No, what I don't get. . . ." His eyes watered. "What I don't get is that he was so good to us, always there for us no matter how busy he was. How could he just forget about his daughter? Family is everything, right?" He looked to them for confirmation.

"Yes," Eileen said, "but we don't know the circumstances. We don't know why Rayna was so angry."

"We have to find his daughter! We have to make sure she's okay, that she's not alone or poor." He stopped. "Mom, did you know about her when you married Dad?"

Eileen shook her head.

"Dad never told you about her?"

There. There was Ivy looking out from her son's eyes, indignant at the injustice of it all.

"I didn't know until I discovered that letter after your dad died. I did try to find Rayna Migielski, but there was no one by that name in the phone book. I didn't take it any further because if she and her daughter had made lives for themselves, bringing up the past might be painful, even destructive, if the other people in their lives didn't know. Now, I know you're angry with your father—I was furious that he'd kept this from me—but there are things about your father's life before we met that you need to know."

Eileen again shared the story of Ivy's early life. Paddy grimaced and a few tears fell at each horrid detail. "I think your father couldn't tell me because he was afraid I would think he was a horrible man and wouldn't marry him."

Paddy pressed his lips together. "Would you have married him?"

"Yes."

"I'm so glad Dad had you—that he had us, too." Then his brow wrinkled and he shook his head. "But I don't understand. Why are you telling me about this now? I mean, you didn't find her. You could have kept this secret, and none of us would ever know."

"Because we have found Ivy's daughter," Shannon said.

Paddy's face burst into a smile that rivaled the sun. "Is she okay? Does she know about us? When are we going to meet her?"

"She's more than okay, and you already know her." Eileen said.

"Huh?"

"She's your mentor."

"My . . . Liz Michaels! No way!" Paddy began laughing so hard, it took him some time to stop. He gasped a final breath, then shook his head. "First day I met her, I noticed the space between her teeth, just like mine. Wow!" He suddenly stopped smiling. "Does she know about us? Does she know I'm her brother?"

"We don't know," said Eileen.

"What if she does know? What if I got the internship because I'm her brother?"

Eileen put on the no-nonsense face they all knew so well. "Paddy, by now, you should have no doubts about your talent and intelligence. And Mrs. Kernan—not Liz Michaels—chose you."

He brightened and nodded his head. "Yeah, okay, Mom. You're—" He stopped and stared, still as a deer sensing a hunter. His mouth dropped open. "I think she does know."

"What makes you think that?" Shannon said.

"When we talked about the space between our teeth, I said it probably reminded Mom of Dad. She didn't think that was so since I didn't look like him. I wondered how she could know that. Then she said that I looked Irish and she assumed that Arnesson was a Swedish name, which meant my dad was probably blond, so I couldn't look like him. I thought it was odd at the time, but I let it go. . . . She knows!"

Eileen covered her mouth with her hand. "Oh my." Then she glanced at Shannon, who said nothing.

"So what do we do now?" Then Paddy grinned. "I know. Let's invite her over for dinner and break the news that we know who she is."

Shannon spoke. "There's more."

Paddy looked from one to the other. "What?"

"Did you hear about her ex-husband?"

"Yeah, people at the company pretty much figured good riddance to bad rubbish. Nobody thought she had anything to do with it. Of course, she never talked about it to me. So what about it?"

"Santello and I worked the case."

"Yeah?"

"Well, when the case was over, Liz and I started seeing each other."

"What! She's the someone you're seeing?" Paddy was momentarily at a loss for words, then he started giggling. "Ew! Uncle Jimmy, you've been dating my sister."

"She's not his niece, Paddy!"

Paddy smirked, his eyes twinkling.

"They're not related, so put a cork in it, mister."

Paddy leaned across the table toward Shannon. "Pervert," he whispered.

"Enough, Paddy!" However, it was all Eileen could do not to laugh at Shannon's white-lipped face. She knew he was thinking about the reaction from the rest of the clan.

Paddy leaned back, his hands palms up in an I-give-up gesture.

"Did you ever mention to her that I was your uncle?"

"No. There's never much time for chit-chat, and, anyway, I didn't want her to think I was a babbling idiot. Mom always told me it was better to say nothing and have people think I was a fool than to prove it by opening my mouth."

The three of them looked at each other. Paddy's eyes misted. "I wish Dad was here for this."

⟨⟨THIRTY-ONE⟩⟩

SHANNON HELD ONTO Eileen's arm as they approached Liz's doors, not that he needed physical support.

"She's done very well for herself, hasn't she?"

"Wait until you see her place."

"Oh, I can imagine. You know, it's a relief to find Ivy's daughter turned out to be better than trailer trash."

Shannon stiffened.

"Oh, you know what I mean. We have a few shady cousins we don't much like. Didn't you arrest one of them once?"

Shannon lost his glare and blushed. "It was a misunderstanding, and we cleared it up."

Eileen grinned and Shannon rang the bell. "Let's hope she doesn't carry her mother's anger."

When the door opened, Liz, in a pale blue cotton dress and sandals, greeted them with a warm smile. "Please come in." She extended her hand. "You must be Eileen. I think I saw you at the hospital."

"Yes, it's a pleasure to meet you, Liz. I hope you don't mind me coming with Jimmy. He's not up to driving yet."

"Of course not. Make yourselves comfortable in the living room. The tea's just about ready."

As they took the three steps down into the living room, Eileen took in the furnishings and the expansive, fairy-twilight view of Pittsburgh. She eyed Shannon and nodded as they sat. In a few moments, Liz reappeared, carrying a silver tray with their tea and a selection of cookies smelling of spice and chocolate. Shannon recognized Steinmetz's best, and his mouth watered.

"You said that it was important that we talk, but you didn't say what about. Is there a problem with Addy's case?" she said as she poured the tea.

"No. That's going ahead without a hitch." Shannon and Eileen focused on sugaring and stirring their tea. Shannon didn't trust himself to touch the cookies—maybe he'd have some later if this went alright. Eileen sipped her tea and gazed into the cup as though it held a more fascinating scene than what was about to play out. He'd like to follow her there, but they'd agreed that he should be the one to tell her.

Liz sat with her cup resting in the palm of her hand, and waited for Shannon to continue. After taking a sip, he put his cup down and smiled at her. "During our investigation, we made an interesting discovery that concerns you."

Liz cocked her head.

"You know we did background checks on everyone. You, too."

She nodded. "And?"

"We know you changed your name. It used to be Migielski."

"Uh-huh, it's really no secret."

Eileen turned to stare at Shannon and nodded him on.

"What would you say if I told you that, because of this investigation, your father's family has discovered you and wants to get to know you?" He clasped his hands together, knuckles turning white, between his knees.

The cup nearly rolled out of Liz's hands. Her face paled. Shannon wanted to go to her and reassure her it would be alright, but he kept his distance.

"I'm sorry. What? My father? How?"

Eileen pulled the letter out of her purse and held it out to Liz. "Please. Read this."

Liz placed her cup on the tray, took the letter with a trembling hand, and stared at the writing on the envelope. "It's from my mother and addressed to. . . ." She looked up at Eileen. "Why do you have this?" She fluttered the envelope against her lap, then stopped. Her eyes widened. "Wait! You! You're his wife! He was afraid . . . he didn't—" Her eyes, like stormy seas, darted from Eileen to Shannon—and remained there. She tensed as though ready to run from a nightmare and gasped. "That means you're my—"

"No! No no! I'm not your uncle. Well, technically, I'm your step-uncle, but that's it. We're not really related."

Liz leaned back into her chair, frowning like she smelled something burning.

"Please. Read the letter. Then we'll talk," coaxed Eileen.

Liz scowled at the woman she believed had kept her father from her and read the yellowed page. Her face reddened. A solitary tear from each eye trailed down her cheeks. Finished, she grabbed a napkin and erased the dampness from her face. "I always knew she was angry with him for getting her pregnant. She even refused to tell me who he was until the day before she died. I was nineteen, and finally the other half of me was no longer a blank."

"Why was she so angry? Ivy must have asked her to marry him." Eileen said.

Liz nodded. "Yes, he did, but my mother said the damage was already done, that she was marked for life. She told me he was being shipped out, and he was scared to death he was going to die. She felt sorry for him. He . . . they . . . she said she wasn't supposed to get pregnant. I think she felt betrayed. I don't know if she loved him, but whatever feelings she had for him died."

Liz now looked like the nineteen-year-old girl she once was. "See, my mother was very sensitive—actually fragile. Apparently, it was tough enough growing up Polish at a time when there was so much discrimination. Seems like she felt she always had to prove she was as good as everyone else, had to be perfect, had to follow all the rules. And then there she was with an illegitimate child. They didn't exactly throw baby showers for those mothers back then."

"Yes, I know. However, she must have realized she wasn't the only woman around in that situation."

Liz tilted her head. "I don't know. I think she had a hard time looking beyond her own misery. Anyway, she said she didn't want to move to Beaver Falls and be stuck on a farm. Didn't want to be judged and snubbed by his father and their neighbors. Besides, he'd told her a few things about his father that scared her. And, well, people in our neighborhood finally stopped talking about her. She didn't want to leave my grandmother alone, either."

"I can't imagine Ivy would have abandoned your grandmother."

Liz shrugged.

"How did your mother die?"

She gazed beyond them. "I don't like to talk about it."

Eileen remained silent.

Liz then brushed her eyes over Eileen. After a moment, she nodded. "She fell from the third-story window of our apartment."

"She fell?"

Liz closed her eyes. "I think she jumped, but there was no way to be sure."

"I'm so sorry. You were only nineteen?"

"Yes." Liz opened her eyes, unaware of her hands twisting and crumpling her napkin. Her voice softened. "Her husband left about a month before, and she'd started drinking. All she did was drink, cry, and sleep. I had to force her to eat. Then one day, I came home from classes and found her sober, clean, and wearing her favorite dress. She even cooked dinner."

Liz stared past them as if seeing the scene. "After we ate, she brought out a box filled with pictures, letters, programs, crumbling corsages, and other odds and ends from when she was young. That's when she told me about my father. So many of the pictures and mementos were from when they were dating. But she also had news clippings about his promotions and family. She kept up with him. I don't know why—maybe for me, in case I needed to find him someday."

"And did you?"

Liz darted her eyes at Eileen, then dropped her gaze to the wadded napkin in her hands. She nodded.

"What happened?"

Liz shook her head without raising her eyes.

"Please, Liz, I need to understand why he didn't bring you home to us."

"Because he didn't want—" She stopped as if reconsidering what she was about to say. "I found your house in Rosslyn Farms but couldn't work up the nerve to knock on your door. So I waited around and hoped he'd come out." She shook her head. "It's so silly. I don't know why I thought he would come out. But he finally did and drove off. I followed him into downtown and met up with him at a diner. He knew I'd been following him and demanded to know why. I told him who I was, and that my mother had just died."

Shannon kept shaking his head, his face stone. Eileen managed to hold back her tears despite the quiver in her lower lip. "What did he say?"

"He was sorry about my mother. He said he wanted to help me, even offered me a job at his insurance company so we could get to know each other. But he said he'd never told anyone about my mother and me, and that he was afraid the news would upset you. He said he loved you and didn't want to hurt you."

"Upset me?" Eileen said, bursting into tears. Shannon put his arm around her until she was able to speak again.

"Well, wouldn't you have been?"

"Oh, yes, for not telling me about you from the beginning. Ivy was quite a few years older than me, had been in the service. I wasn't so naïve as to think he didn't have some history. He did tell me all about his childhood, about the girl he almost married, about some of his experiences in the war."

"Would you have married him if you knew about me?"

"Yes. But first, I would have made him go to Rayna—to be sure she was alright, to make sure she hadn't changed her mind about marrying him. And if she still wanted nothing to do with him, to persuade her that it was important for him to be in your life."

"Wouldn't you have resented me for being there?"

Eileen looked at Liz like she didn't understand the question. "Resent you? Your father was the love of my life. How could I resent his child?"

"Rudy, my step-father, always acted like I was in the way. Then he left my mother, so I guess she wasn't the love of his life."

Eileen lowered her eyes to the rings on her fingers.

Shannon, still stone-faced, shook his head. "How did you manage all alone at nineteen?"

"My mother and Rudy had some savings, and there was the insurance money. I was also working part time for the Kernans when they had their print shop."

"But you were all alone!" Eileen said.

"Not for long. The Kernans took me in. They insisted I live with them until I finished college. So I did end up with a family after all."

Eileen shook her head. "We should have been your family. When I found that letter after Ivy died, I tried to find your mother, but there were no Migielskis in the phone book. I thought perhaps she'd married, and maybe you even had your own family. I didn't want to create any problems, so I let it go." Her eyes became moist again. "How I wish he had told me."

Liz's eyes softened at Eileen's disappointment. "Miriam Kernan and I talked about this shortly after Paddy became one of our interns." She smiled at Eileen and shook her head. "I couldn't believe the odds of one of you ending up at Kernan, Feinstein and Company. Anyway, Miriam helped me see that he really hadn't rejected me. She reminded me he made the job offer to get to know me. But you see, back then, I was so hurt that he didn't want anyone to know I was his daughter, I didn't give him a chance. I ran out of that diner and never turned back."

"He should have run after you," said Shannon.

Eileen nodded in agreement, then stopped. "He must have been so torn. On one hand, he had a daughter he should have taken into his home, and on the other, he had a wife and family he thought he might lose." She looked at Liz through puffy eyes. "Your father was a very sad man when I met him. He'd had such a terrible life. When I thought about all he'd gone through, I was finally able to understand his fear and forgive him."

"What happened to him?"

Eileen glanced at Shannon, eased back in her chair, and then shared Ivy's past with his daughter.

When Eileen finished, Liz shook her head. "How awful."

"Oh, what he had with us more than made up for the past. He had the acceptance and love of the Shannon clan and his own family. He became a different man—always laughing and joking."

"Yeah, he was quite a prankster. I should know because I was often the target of his pranks—but he was never mean," Shannon said.

"I can see how he thought he had so much to lose."

"But he lost you." Eileen rose, crossed to Liz, sat on the arm of her chair and put her arms around her. "But we're not going to miss out on you anymore. I hope you'll want to meet the rest of your family."

Shannon chuckled. "And she's not just talking about the three sisters you haven't met. When Eileen says family, she means aunts, uncles, cousins, their kids, their parents, their spouses' relatives—you may find the entire population of Pittsburgh is your family."

Eileen raised an eyebrow at him. "He's exaggerating."

Liz chuckled and then gazed at the tea service. "You know, I really didn't want to mentor Paddy. I was afraid I'd let slip who I was, experience more rejection. But Miriam assigned him to me and insisted it would be a good thing. By the way, does he know?"

Both Shannon and Eileen nodded and smiled.

"I think he was happier about finding out you're his sister than he was when he got published in *Penwell*, although he did give me a hard time about dating his sister."

Liz let out a breath. "This has been quite a shock, to say the least. I'm really going to need some time to digest all of this."

Eileen took Liz's hand. "We all need time, but please don't run away from us, Liz. We're your family."

Liz smiled and nodded, and Eileen hugged her.

Eileen decided to wait for Shannon in the lobby. He and Liz stood at her door. They didn't speak and looked everywhere but at each other. Finally, Liz glanced at him. "Awkward, isn't it?" she said.

Shannon nodded. "Yeah, finding out who you are really rocked me. I wondered what we should do."

"I know. Should we continue seeing each other?"

So she hasn't closed the door on this yet.

"I sure would like to, but then there's this family business. It won't be easy."

Liz nodded.

Shannon took her hands and gazed into her eyes. He wanted to kiss her, but he wanted her to have the distance she needed right now. So he smiled and gently squeezed her hands. "Looks like we both have a lot to keep us awake tonight."

"Yes, it does."

He didn't want to let go of her hands, but he knew he had to. "Well, good night."

He drifted down the hall and pressed the button for the elevator. He gazed back at her door in deep thought and startled when she popped into the hall and hurried up to him with a Steinmetz box.

"Here, take the cookies. You didn't get a chance to eat any."

"Thanks." He took the box, and just as the elevator arrived, she caught his face with one hand and kissed his cheek. They smiled at each other, and he entered the elevator. The doors closed. After they finally opened to the lobby, he still felt the softness of her lips on his face. If he hadn't been handicapped by a box of cookies, he would have kissed her the way he'd wanted to all evening. Shannon wondered how it would all turn out.

Liz sauntered into the break room for coffee and Danish the next morning and discovered Paddy sitting at one of the tables. He glanced up and they smiled at each other. He looked into his mug and then back up at her. He shrugged his shoulders, still smiling. She wondered if he'd been waiting for her.

"Hi."

She dipped her head and sat. "So how do you feel about all of this?"

His grin widened. "I'm feeling like it's Christmas morning and the Fourth of July."

Liz laughed.

"How about you?" he said.

"Mm, I think I'm still recovering from the shock."

He lost his smile. "Oh?"

"Oh, I'm glad to finally connect with all of you. It's just . . . well, your uncle. . . . It's a little awkward."

"Oh, no biggie."

"And there are your sisters and the rest of your mother's family. What will they think of all of this, especially if your uncle and I continue to see each other?"

"They'll be happy for him, so don't think you have to stop seeing him. Anyway, they'll think you're terrific, just like I do. In fact, I'm honored to have you for my sister."

Liz smiled. "Thank you. The feeling's mutual. But I think it's going to be very unpleasant—at the very least, awkward—for your mother when she tells everyone about me. Won't they wonder about the man she married keeping something so important from her?"

"Well, it's not like he was cheating on her. He and Mom didn't meet until long after your mother ended their relationship."

"But he wasn't honest with her."

"Mom told me about his childhood. None of us knew anything more about his past other than that he was an only child, grew up on a farm around Beaver Falls, and his parents died before he met Mom. She said he wanted to protect us from all the ugly parts of his life, that, as far as he was concerned, his life really began when he met her. I got it."

"Still, it won't be easy for her."

"Hey, don't worry about Mom. She's the family wise woman."

Liz cocked her head and looked at him.

"You know, every family has one—a wise woman or wise man, the go-to person when you have a problem. Everybody respects her. Seeing how she handles our situation will probably convince them she's a candidate for sainthood." Then Paddy looked at her seriously. "No, my only concern is that you'll be overwhelmed by all of them. They're quite a crew."

Liz grimaced.

He pulled several sheets of paper and photos out of a folder. "I've listed most of them with a little explanation of who they are and what they're like. I started with my sisters. The oldest is Siobhan. Here's her picture. That's her husband Joe and their two kids Rachel and Dustin. We all call her 'Vonnie.' She's the manager of commercial lines underwriting at the same insurance company where Dad worked. She's a little bossy, but I guess that goes with being the oldest. She concerns me the most. See, if she likes you, you have a champion for life. If she doesn't, well, she'll act like you're invisible."

He pointed at another photo of a man and a sweet-faced young woman who resembled Eileen and Vonnie. "And then there's Erin. She's Director of Personnel at Shannon Trucking. The guy next to her is her husband Walt. They don't have any kids, yet. Erin's pretty quiet. When she was little, she was always rescuing baby birds, even grasshoppers. She even rescued a cat from a sewer drain and brought it home. Mom told her no more animals after that."

The next photo showed a whimsical, elfin girl with riotous dark curls. "This is my other sister Maura. She's an artist in the graphics department at the *Post Gazette*. She paints, too, and has had a few showings. She's not married. Vonnie thinks she's a little ditzy, but Maura is just one of those people who lives in the moment and finds everything just great."

Liz noticed that none of them resembled Ivar Arnesson. They all shared Eileen's dark hair and pert Irish features.

Paddy told her more about the girls' past. She nodded and asked an occasional question. Her little brother then guided her through the remaining jumble of relatives she would soon meet.

$\xi \gamma c \gamma c \varphi$

"And how did Paddy take the news?" Miriam asked. She signaled the waiter for more coffee.

Liz smiled, remembering their review session that morning. "He told me how honored—that's the word he used—how honored he was to have me as his sister. He was so funny this morning. He was afraid I might be overwhelmed by the whole clan, so he felt it his duty to give me the lowdown on all of the family I was likely to meet, complete with cheat sheet and pictures. They're an interesting lot. There's even a cousin—Brigit I think her name is—who has predictive dreams."

She wrinkled her brow. "Eileen phoned later this morning about setting up a time to meet her three daughters after she breaks the news to them." Liz sighed and shook her head. "Miriam, this is all so bizarre."

"It's not as bizarre as you think. I could tell you many stories of far stranger reunions after World War II in the refugee camps. I expected—hoped—you would eventually unite with your father's family. The detective? I call him a bonus. It was meant to be. One way or another, you are destined to be part of that family," Miriam said.

They finished their late lunch at Vinaigrette. Few of the lunch crowd remained, and the servers bothered them only to warm their coffee and remove their plates. No glowering clutch of women manned any of the tables this day.

"Destined? I don't know. It's all so very awkward. She must have loved him very much to have forgiven him for not telling her. Of course, after she told me about my father's childhood and how he changed when he joined their family, I could see why he was so fearful when I tracked him down. Maybe I should have given him another chance."

"But it's all worked out."

"I don't know."

"What is it you don't know, *Liebling*?"

Liz frowned. "It's complicated. I have a chance to get to know my father's family, maybe to be included." She thought of Siobhan. "Although some of them may not like me. But . . .

why must there always be a 'but'? Jim is also a part of that family."

"And?"

"Won't it be awkward? Especially at family gatherings?"

"Family gatherings often make for uncomfortable encounters. Everyone manages one way or another. What matters is what is important to the two of you. It wasn't easy for Gerald and me, but we were too important to each other to let the disapproval of others pull us apart." Miriam covered Liz's hand. "Perhaps you are creating problems where none exist."

"What do you mean?"

"Only that you may be afraid to risk another relationship after Addy. You have become quite comfortable living alone, but life is so much sweeter shared with the right person."

"What if he's not the right person?"

Miriam smiled. "You won't know for sure unless you get to know him better. You've been greatly hurt and disappointed, lost a child. Now you are a wiser woman, not the young thing who was so awed by Addy's background and education. That little voice in your heart has already told you that you can expect better from the detective. Don't let fear muzzle your wiser instincts."

҉THIRTY–TWO҉

SANTELLO, MOUTH OPEN, scalded her hand when she jostled the heavy mug of steaming coffee. She slammed the mug on Eileen's kitchen table and wiped her reddening hand with the napkin. A giggle gurgled deep in her throat before erupting into a Vesuvius of laughter. Catching her breath, she looked at him straight-faced. "Seamus Aloysius, you're dating your niece!" She burst into laughter again.

"First, Paddy. Now, you. I'm getting a little tired of hearing that. We're really not related."

Santello shook her head, still laughing. "Wait 'til the guys at the station hear about it. And the rest of your family? Woo-hoo!"

Shannon, unsmiling, said nothing.

"Oh, don't look so glum. Just like me, once they all get over the initial shock, they'll get a kick out of it. Be prepared. It will probably help if you laugh about it instead of looking so defensive." She retrieved a couple of ice cubes from the freezer and dumped them in her coffee. "Your sister is something else. Any other woman would be furious with her husband keeping mum about a child he'd fathered."

"Yeah, even though Eileen's all about unconditional love, you'd think she'd really be upset. But you never knew Ivy. He had a childhood straight out of one of those dismal Swedish films. He was an only child, and his parents were Swedish immigrants who had a farm in Beaver Falls. Any relatives were either dead or in Sweden."

"What's so bad about that?"

Shannon told her the story of Ivy's early life, and by the time he finished, Santello's features wilted like last Sunday's altar flowers.

She shook her head. "Poor guy."

"Eileen wasn't happy that he didn't trust her love for him. She really believes in 'for better or worse,' and wouldn't have married any man she couldn't promise that to. She loved him. Period. At first, she found it hard to forgive him, but she soon realized that the losses earlier in his life led him to expect the worst."

"Yeah, if he'd told her, you might have gotten to know Liz earlier, but then you'd probably always think of her as one of your nieces, even if you are only a few years older. No chance at romance then. So how's that going?"

"I guess you'd say we have a lot to think about."

"What do you mean? What's to think about?"

"The chemistry's there, but it's still early in the game. What if it doesn't work out? What if we end up despising each other? Then there's the family."

Santello sighed and shook her head. "You know, Seamus Aloysius, your talent for considering all the 'what ifs' makes you a great detective, but you can't let it cripple you when it comes to living your life. There are all kinds of risks to anything worth having. I should know. Getting involved with Mona was pretty risky since she'd never really had a lesbian relationship before meeting me, but look what we ended up having. I wouldn't have missed it for the world."

Shannon nodded.

"By the way, when will Bugielski let you get back to work, although the Captain will probably make you a desk jockey until you're fully healed and your psych evaluation is completed?"

"It really doesn't matter. Once all the worker's comp and medical paperwork is done, I'm resigning. I haven't changed my mind."

You can't leave the force, Shannon! You are too good a detective. It's like a calling—you know, the way priests and nuns have a calling. You can't turn your back on it. God won't let you. Mark my words, if you try to leave, He'll yank you right back."

Shannon did not respond immediately. Then he sighed. "Getting shot like that, not knowing it was coming, not remembering—and that kid ending up dead, too, because of some misplaced loyalty to his no-good brother. I'm burned out, Santello. I can't look at one more bruised and bloodied woman, one more starved-to-death child, one more dead sixteen-year-old addict, one more criminal getting off on a technicality. We have to weave through so many mazes to get justice." He shook his head. "I'm not drinking day in and day out yet, and I'm nowhere near wanting to eat my gun, but enough is enough. I'm finished."

"That means there will be one less committed detective to stand up for those victims. Maybe we barely make a dent in the evil we see, but without good cops like you, it would be much worse, really much worse, Shannon."

He nodded. Neither of them spoke for awhile. Santello sniffed the aroma of chocolate and spices, reached into the Steinmetz box, and retrieved a large almond cookie. "So where's Eileen?"

"She took the girls out to dinner. She's going to tell them about Liz."

Her eyes twinkled. Maybe with Liz in his life, in time, he'd feel different about doing the job he was born to do. She had no doubt something would happen to open his eyes to the truth. She nibbled at the butter-rich cookie and sipped her coffee, which had finally cooled to her liking.

ξㅜ당

Her three girls, their mouths open, reminded Eileen of a nest of hungry baby birds. Only, they had to be quite sated after eating the exquisite fare of The Terrace Room. At Eileen's request, they sat at a secluded table in the William Penn Hotel's famed restaurant. She'd told them she'd found an important letter among his things after their father died and gave it to them to read. They squeezed together to read it at the same time. Finished, they sat looking at her for answers to questions they couldn't yet put into words. Then she told them about Liz and how Shannon met her.

Vonnie was the first to recover. "Mom, how do you know she's Dad's daughter? You don't really know anything about her mother." She shook the letter. "Maybe this woman was lying. She might be someone else's daughter."

"Vonnie, why would Rayna write him, especially to tell him she didn't want anything to do with him, if Liz wasn't his child? Besides, when you meet her, you'll have no doubts. She's the spitting image of your father. She even has that gap between her teeth. All of you took after me. Other than Paddy having that same gap between his teeth, none of you bear a strong resemblance to your dad."

Vonnie pressed her lips together and drew a noisy breath through pinched nostrils.

"Why didn't Dad tell you about them, Mom?" I don't get it," Maura, her youngest girl, said.

"I can't say it didn't hurt me that he kept something so important from me. As a matter of fact, I was furious for quite some time. Remember, you all kept asking me if I was okay back then?"

"Yeah, we thought you were depressed. It worried us." Erin said. The others nodded.

Well, I thought about his past and came to realize why he was so fearful. Liz told me she had tracked him down when her mother died in 1965. He told her that he loved all of us so much and was afraid he would lose us if he told me about her."

"What about his past, Mom?" Vonnie said.

"Wait! You mean he just turned his back on her? Right after her mother died?" Erin interrupted.

"Fear has a way of blinding people, Erin." Eileen looked down at her plate. "In truth, fear is the root of all evil."

Vonnie interrupted before Erin could go on. "I still want to know about Dad's past."

Eileen turned back to them. "Okay. You're not children any more." She looked at each of them and then told them about their father's horrific childhood and early years. "He told me he didn't remember his father hitting his mother, but sometimes children blank out what they don't want to see," she said at the end.

"Oh, Daddy," whispered Erin, her eyes glistening. "Oh, I'm so glad Dad had you—and us."

"He was glad, too. He was so serious when we first met, and I sensed sadness in him. Of course, I understood why after he told me about his past. At first, he was really overwhelmed by us Shannons. I was afraid we were too much for him, but it wasn't long before he relaxed and jumped in with both feet. You all remember what a joker he was. Well, that side of him bloomed with us."

Maura cackled.

Vonnie looked at her youngest sister. "What?"

"I was just thinking of some of the gags Dad pulled."

Vonnie rolled her eyes. "What I don't understand is why Liz's mother didn't want to have anything to do with him."

Eileen repeated everything that Liz had learned from her mother.

"Poor Dad. What's with these women? I don't understand how anyone could not love him," Maura said.

Vonnie shook her head. "Always the romantic. Maura, just because we adored Dad, doesn't mean every woman he ever knew would fall head over heels for him."

Maura pushed back from the table and looked down at her hands.

Erin raised her eyebrows. "Vonnie."

Vonnie huffed and looked back at their mother. "So, she's a bigwig in this publishing firm?"

Eileen regarded her oldest daughter a moment. She should have expected Vonnie to be prickly, but she'd hoped she would be more accepting. "Yes, despite everything, she's made quite a success of herself."

Vonnie leaned back in her chair. "How did that happen?"

"She worked for the other owners of Kernan, Feinstein and Company when they ran a print shop in Carnegie. After her mother died, they—the Kernans—insisted she live with them until she graduated from Pitt. They were in the process of starting their publishing company at the time, and when she graduated, she continued working for them. Their son and daughter had no interest in the business, and Liz apparently did a great deal to make it a success, so they made her part owner."

"I'm so glad there was somebody who cared about her. Who knows what might have happened to her if there hadn't been anybody," Erin said.

Vonnie rolled her eyes again, a habit she'd developed in adolescence and never outgrown. Eileen ignored her and nodded at Erin. They all sat quietly, lost in their own thoughts.

Finally, Eileen broke the silence. "You know, our cousin Brigit told me she dreamed we had four daughters and a son. She said you all would look like me except for one of the girls. It baffled her to no end that we only had you three and Paddy and none of you looked like your dad. She thought we should keep trying for a fourth girl. She'll be tickled to learn that her dream wasn't quite so wrong."

Vonnie looked at her mother, unsmiling. "Does Paddy know who she is?"

Eileen laughed. "Yes, and he's as happy as a fly in honey. You see, she's his mentor at the publishing company. Since the day he met her, he's had nothing but admiration for her. He'd also noticed that she has the same space between her teeth that he has."

Erin and Maura, smiling, shook their heads.

Vonnie remained unsmiling. "Unbelievable! Did she know who Paddy was?"

"Yes, and she never let on that they were related." Before Vonnie could ask, Eileen continued. "And, no, he did not get the internship because he was her brother."

Vonnie thinks she's losing her place as the big sister. So silly. They all grew up together. The others would always look to her as their big sister. Eileen had every confidence that her very bright eldest daughter would eventually tumble to that.

Maura whooped, and they all looked at her like she'd grown an extra nose. "You know what's unbelievable?" They all waited. "If Uncle Jim hadn't been the detective on her case and got interested in her, we might never have known about her.

"Maybe that would've been a good thing," Vonnie said.

Eileen gave her "the look," and Vonnie said nothing more. She then placed her hand over Vonnie's and softened her gaze to assure her that all would be well. Vonnie relaxed into a brief smile and nodded.

After the waiter cleared their table and brought the bill, Erin asked when they would meet Liz.

"I thought a brunch at the house this Saturday would work. Liz said she could make it then. That's a day off for all of you, and everybody should be rested."

They all agreed.

"Does the rest of the family know yet? And that Uncle Jim is seeing her?" Erin asked.

"Your Aunt Fiona is handling that. She's using the telephone tree."

Vonnie slapped the table with both hands. "Oh my God! By the time the last ones on the tree get called, the message will be she's Siamese twins selling magazines at a corner newsstand!"

ɕⲧⲧTHIRTY–THREE ⲧⲉⳃ

ADELAIDE HAUSER SAVORED her morning breakfast and lingered at the solid maple kitchen table. The midmorning sun glimmered through the tall kitchen windows, and the aroma of coffee, bacon, and eggs enveloped her. She was able to start her mornings later these days, which made the ritual even more enjoyable. She drank the last of her coffee and peered at the kitchen clock. It was after nine, time for her to do the weekly shopping. Mrs. Payne had not stirred and would probably still be asleep upon her return.

She had been keeping a close eye on the woman since her son's funeral. When Detective Shannon called to explain to Mrs. Payne how Addy had died, she merely thanked him and hung up. Adelaide waited for the fireworks, but the woman only sat there and stared into space with flinty eyes. Since that call, she rarely left the house, accepted few calls, slept until noon, and ate little. And instead of an occasional glass of wine, she now downed several glasses of gin and tonic daily. Adelaide began hiding the key to the liquor cabinet and reporting it lost, but invariably she would have to find it before the rising storm in Mrs. Payne's eyes broke into a full-blown, thundering torrent. Otherwise, too many pieces of good china and crystal lost their lives to the trash can.

Adelaide wrung her hands as she witnessed the well-groomed woman regress into a crone, her once lustrous pageboy a scraggly mess surrounding a face totally devoid of care and cosmetic enhancement. And she either wore her night gown day in and day out or slept in the same clothes until Adelaide would gently suggest she might enjoy a relaxing soak in the tub and a fresh change of clothes.

All of this concerned Adelaide, but what worried her more was the raging sea of grief that engulfed Eunice Payne, releasing her from its depths only long enough to curse Liz Michaels. Day by day, the invectives grew worse and more frequent. Adelaide often heard her scream, "You killed my dear, precious boy, you trashy, pasty-faced bitch, and you'll pay! I'll make sure you pay!" That's when Adelaide began regularly checking the desk drawer containing the gun. She thought about hiding it, but its disappearance would not have been as easy to explain as a misplaced liquor cabinet key.

She had called Eunice's brother and sister-in-law, but they were not concerned, saying she would work through her grief without any interference from them. Besides, they knew Adelaide would look after her. So she watched, hoping the woman would finally reach some island of peace and stay there.

Adelaide rinsed her breakfast dishes and placed them in the dishwasher. She grabbed her purse and reached for the keys to the Mercedes, but they weren't on the hook where they were always kept. A quick inspection of the counter and floor revealed no keys. She opened the drawers, thinking she might have thrown them into one. She was getting to the age when she sometimes misplaced things. Again, no keys. Adelaide's breathing quickened. Where could those keys be?

The garage was just off the kitchen. She thrust the door open and immediately saw that only her old Chevy station wagon occupied the huge garage, and the garage door was open. Had someone stolen the car? She had made sure the house was secure last night.

Banging the door shut, Adelaide fled down the hall, bumping against a console. Climbing the stairs two at a time, she yelled Mrs. Payne's name but heard no answer. She found what she feared she would when she opened the bedroom door.

Empty.

Maybe she couldn't sleep and went for a drive. Was that a ridiculous thought?

How could her stomach feel so hollow after such a good breakfast? Adelaide knew she had to check one more place.

She flew down the stairs only slightly slower than she had climbed them and paused at the entrance to the den. The chart and insurance policy had never left the surface of the desk. The desk chair, however, was pushed back.

Oh no! No. Please let it be there.

She rushed to the desk and found the drawer containing the gun chest hanging open and the lid of the chest flung back.

The gun was gone.

There was only one place Mrs. Payne would go with that gun. It was Friday, and Liz Michaels would probably be at work. Could Mrs. Payne already be there? She might be if she had left at dawn. What to do? What to do?

Adelaide doubted she could find the grieving woman before she did something horrible. Besides, she now carried a loaded gun, and Adelaide had no desire to make herself a target. What had she done with that detective's number?

She ran to her room, rifled the drawers of her tiny secretary, and found the card. She grabbed the phone and dialed.

"Homicide Division, Detective Santello speaking."

"Who? What? Where's Detective Shannon?"

"Detective Shannon is unavailable, and I'm handling his calls. How may I help you?"

"I, uh . . . I, uh . . ."

"Who's calling, please?"

Adelaide did not respond.

"Look, I'm Detective Shannon's partner. I can assure you that whatever you need from him, I can help you with."

"Yes, yes, of course. I'm Adelaide Hauser, Mrs. Payne's housekeeper. Detective Shannon worked on Addison Payne's case. Mrs. Payne is his mother."

"Uh-huh. Detective Shannon and I both worked that case. You sound upset. What can I do for you, Ms. Hauser?"

Adelaide pushed on her stomach, trying to arrest the encroaching heartburn. "It's Mrs. Payne. . . . She has a gun! You've got to stop her!"

"Calm down, Ms. Hauser. Where is Mrs. Payne now?"

"I'm not sure. I think she is wherever Ms. Michaels is, probably at her publishing company."

"What makes you think that?"

"She's been such a mess since her son died, and she blames the Michaels woman even though it was that bartender who poisoned him. And . . . and . . . oh, I should have told somebody about this before now."

"What, Ms. Hauser?"

"Mrs. Payne found a chart and an insurance policy at her son's place. The policy was on Liz Michaels, and the chart . . . the chart made me think he was planning to kill her. And now, Mrs. Payne is so out of her mind with grief, I think she's going to do it."

"I'll take care of this, Ms. Hauser. In the meantime, please bring that policy and the chart into the station. Can you do that?"

"Yes. Please, you must stop her. She's sick. She's not in her right mind."

⇐ ⟡ ⟡ ⟡ ⇒

Eunice had never driven so fast in her entire life. The highway gods were with her this morning. Traffic was light, and not a police car was in sight. The Mercedes handled the speeds well.

Tears no longer streaked her now granite face. She wondered why it had taken her so long to get going and do what she had to do. Thank God, she answered the call from Elaine. Elaine described Liz's laughter and chatter at Vinaigrette in motion-picture detail.

How dare that woman enjoy herself when the sun would never again shine on Addy's sweet face. It was all her fault that he was driven to such extreme measures, and she would pay. Eunice reached over and patted the purse on the seat next to her.

"Dear, dear Addy, I'm going to balance the score for you today, honey. A life for a life."

A life. There had been another child long before her precious Addy. But that child had been ripped from her seventeen-year-old body in a bright, sterile Swiss clinic.

Eunice had loved her blond, god-like tennis coach beyond reason, even though he could not lay claim to wealth and a family name matching her own. After the abortion, her mother sailed Eunice's empty body back to their home. The darling tennis coach was gone, and no one—absolutely no one—could tell her where he'd gone.

A few years later, Jonathan Payne, a member of the right crowd, entered her life. She didn't love him but married him anyway. She'd met no one else she who could fill the crater created by her two losses, and the match thrilled her parents. But more precious to her than the wealth and class Jonathan represented was the son he gave her. Addy was everything to her—the lost baby, the lost lover, her lost self.

Killing that nobody woman won't bring him back, but at least she'll no longer be around to enjoy the fruits of Addy's labor. She pounded the steering wheel.

Oh that I should have lived to see this child dead, too!

Eunice blinked her eyes, refusing to give in to the pain. Pittsburgh was only a few more miles away.

❦

"Come on, come on, pick up, Liz!" Santello slammed down the phone. "Too damned busy to answer the phone."

She could try the main number, but her gut told her she needed to get to Liz pronto. "Korpielsky, I need you for back-up." She glanced at her substitute partner. "Johnny, you stay here and keep trying this number for Liz Michaels and tell her to get out of the office and hide. Try the other numbers for the company, too, and tell whoever answers to alert security to be on the lookout for an old woman by the name of Eunice Payne and to lock down the building. We have a mad-woman gunning for Michaels."

༄༄༄

After the third time the phone rang, Liz unplugged it. Reception could take a message. She only needed two unin-terrupted hours to get her desk cleared. Whatever the callers wanted could wait that long.

༄༄༄

Eunice Payne, in wrinkled slacks and oxford shirt, still wearing slippers, breezed by the receptionist busy on the phone and entered the elevator before the security guard noticed her. It wouldn't be long now. Addy would be avenged. Her heart lightened at the thought.

When she exited the elevator, she noted there were few people around. Being a Friday near the end of summer, peo-ple were probably taking long weekends. Michaels' assistant was absent from her desk, too. Good. One less obstacle to deal with. She strode toward Liz's office.

༄༄༄

Liz, deep in thought over the manuscript in front of her, startled back in her chair when Eunice slammed the door open. It took a moment to register that the sallow-skinned, sunken-eyed, disheveled woman standing in the doorway was Eunice Payne.

"Eunice?"

Her former mother-in-law slid into the room as effortlessly and purposefully as a water moccasin. "Hello, Liz."

Liz felt the hairs on her neck stand up. "Eunice, are you alright? Why don't you have a seat, and I'll get you some tea."

"Oh no. You aren't going anywhere." Eunice grinned as she pulled the gun from her purse.

Liz gaped at the gun, feeling her pulse race and her heart beating in her ears. The room began to turn gray before she got control of herself. "Killing me isn't going to bring Addy back."

"No, but you'll be dead, too. You won't be enjoying any more gourmet dinners. No more designer clothes." She glanced around the office. "No nice job."

Liz edged toward the side door to the hall leading to the fire stairs.

"Don't move!"

"Or what? You'll shoot me?"

They were both stunned when the side door to the hall crashed open revealing Santello and Korpielsky. Both had their guns drawn.

"Gun on the floor and hands up!" Santello yelled.

Recovering, Eunice took aim at Liz. Santello leaped in front of Liz as all three guns fired. Santello fell back onto Liz, taking them both down; and Eunice crumpled to the floor, blood pouring from two wounds, one to her chest and one to her head.

Korpielsky rushed to Eunice, kicked the gun away from her, and checked for a pulse he knew he wouldn't find when he looked into the blank staring eyes in the woman's face.

"Santello. You good?"

"She's bleeding badly. We need to get her help!"

Korpielsky reached for the phone and found it dead. He looked to Liz for help.

"You have to plug it in," she said.

Liz held Santello in her arms, paying no attention to the widening pool of blood surrounding them. "Rose? Rose, please hang on."

Santello looked up at Liz. Her eyes widened and softened as though she recognized someone.

"Mona?"

❦THIRTY-FOUR❧

SOMEONE TOUCHED HIS shoulder and whispered his name. Shannon opened his eyes and, for a moment, couldn't remember where he was. Then he realized he was on the recliner with Eileen's copy of James Lee Burke's *Two for Texas* on his lap. He grinned. "Sorry, Ei. Thought I'd rest my eyes for just a minute." He saw McIlheny hovering a few feet away. "Captain?"

McIlheny nodded. "Shannon." Seeing Shannon struggling to free himself from the recliner, he said, "Don't get up." He sat in the armchair across from Shannon while Eileen sat in the other. "How are you feeling?"

"Tired mostly, but pretty good, considering."

McIlheny nodded and then studied the pattern in the carpet. Eileen sat quietly, her hands in her lap, glancing at each of them in turn. Shannon lost his welcoming smile and clutched the book on his lap.

"What's up, Cap?"

McIlheny swept his gaze back to Shannon. "We had an incident this morning. Addison Payne's mother went after Ms. Michaels with a gun."

Shannon lost his grip on the book. "Liz?" was all he could get out.

"She's okay. She's at the home of the other partners in her company. They're taking care of her."

Shannon closed his eyes, and his heart slowed. He opened them. "What happened? You aren't here just to tell me she's okay. You could have told me that over the phone."

The slender, gray-haired man gazed down at the carpet again, shaking his head. He looked up. "The reason Ms. Michaels is okay is because Santello took a bullet for her."

"She what! She at Mercy?" Trying to free himself from the recliner, he looked at Eileen. "Ei, I've got to be there." But she didn't move to help him, instead she burst into tears. Barely breathing, he turned to stare at McIlheny.

The police captain stared back, saying nothing. Then he nodded.

Shannon crumpled back into the recliner. His eyes rested on the dust motes floating in the early afternoon sunlight streaming through the windows. Images of Santello flashed before him—cuffing a perp with a self-satisfied smirk; her short, compact body striding to an interrogation room; smiling in satisfaction as she drank coffee long past the cool stage; her cackling laughter at a joke she'd just told that no one else found funny; her professorial posturing as she explained a theory to him.

He shook his head. Oh, how he would miss hearing her call him "Seamus Aloysius" whenever she thought he was being stupid, like she had last night when she again tried to convince him he belonged on the force.

His partner—his friend—had died to protect the woman who might eventually become a very important part of his life. Santello saved her by acting as she always had; an unflinching member of that breed of cops who were true warriors.

And that's what she thought he was—a protector, one who would pursue justice for victims at any cost; not someone who would drown in drink and eat his gun in despair. Shannon had sworn to protect and serve, but would he have done the same in her shoes? He touched his face and found it wet. He let the tears fall freely.

❦

Liz lay on plump, flowered cushions in the Kernan's backyard gazebo, shaded from the afternoon sun. The sound of the sliding door awakened her. Her dream of her grandmother and mother whispering, "Don't lose him," faded, but the scent of vanilla remained, a counterpoint to the subtle fragrance of roses.

Shannon, tieless and the sleeves of his white shirt rolled up, navigated the paths through Gerald Kernan's many prize roses. He was such a beautiful man, even though he was still pale and walked like he was making his way over an icy sidewalk. As he got closer, she couldn't help tensing. How could she face him when she was the reason Santello was dead? There was nothing she could say that would change that.

He scaled the three steps into the gazebo and sank into the cushions across from her. His face looked thinner, and the creases around his eyes made him look like he hadn't gotten much sleep. He didn't smile, and she waited for him to tell her that he thought it best they not see each other. She could understand. She had been thinking the same thing herself.

"I'm glad you're staying with the Kernans for awhile. You shouldn't be alone after something like that."

Her eyes grew large, and she began to tremble. She finally burst into tears so intense, she could only gasp. Shannon hurried to her side and took her into his arms, wincing slightly from the pressure on his healing wound.

"Hey, hey," he crooned as he began rocking her. "That's right. Just let it out. Let it go."

Her grief was for Rose, for him, and for all the losses of her own life—family, baby, the dream of a life together with Addy. She listened to his beating heart and inhaled the faint spicy scent of his aftershave. She felt like she had always belonged in his arms. This was home, and she wanted to stay there forever. She wondered if she could remain the independent person she'd become, yet live her life with someone by her side. Someone like Jim Shannon. No. Not someone like him.

Him.

However, it was an empty hope that tore at her heart. Jim Shannon was a kind man, so of course, he would respond like this. She mustn't lose sight of the fact that she was responsible for his partner's death. She knew she'd never forget it, so how could he?

"I'm sorry. I'm so sorry."

"Sh."

"It's all my fault."

His arm still around her, he looked into her eyes. "Why do you think it's your fault?"

Liz looked away, her eyes alighting on a fully-bloomed, wine-hued rose. "If I had answered my phone instead of turning it off, I could have gotten out of my office before Eunice showed up. Then Rose wouldn't have gotten shot. But no! I had to have my uninterrupted couple of hours! And I didn't lock my door like I usually do! With so many people gone, I didn't think anyone would bother me. So stupid!" She turned back to him. "I'm the one who should be dead."

Shannon shook his head. "Look, what you're feeling right now? I'm feeling that, too, even though there was nothing I could have done about it. Ernie Korpielsky is probably feeling the same thing, running the scenario through his head, playing it different ways to find one way where nobody got hurt. But it's no good. In police work, twenty-twenty hindsight doesn't even help you in future situations. Every situation is different. And Korpielsky will have to prove to Internal Affairs that shooting Eunice Payne was the only way it could have gone down."

He took her hands in his. "Do I wish Rose wasn't dead? With every breath. Would I rather you were dead instead? No way."

Looking down at her hands clasped in his, Liz shook her head. "Every time you look at me, you'll remember that Rose died because of me."

Shannon turned her face toward him. "Rose Santello was a professional. She took an oath to serve and protect, and that's just what she did. She was the best of the best, and did the only thing she could do. She did it for her partner before me and got shot, she did for me and didn't get hit, and she did it for you. If she'd survived, she'd go on protecting those around her, no matter the cost."

His tired eyes held nothing but kindness and concern for her. He smiled and nodded, then the smile disappeared. "There's something you should know."

Liz held her breath.

"We now know what Payne was doing in your place. Captain McIlheny told me that when Miss Hauser called to warn us about Mrs. Payne, she said she had some documents that belonged to your ex-husband. Rose told her to bring them in."

"What were they?"

"One was a life insurance policy on you with him as the beneficiary. The other was a flow chart for his business startup. Your name was on it, and it was pretty clear he intended you to die that day."

"He . . . Addy was going to kill me?"

Shannon nodded.

Liz shook her head and searched out the blooms in the garden as if they could make sense of it. "How?" She was at a loss to say more.

"When she and Mrs. Payne cleared out Payne's apartment, they took his briefcase. Mrs. Payne found the papers inside."

"Why didn't Adelaide report it sooner?"

Shannon shrugged. "I'm guessing she didn't think it was worth stirring the pot since Payne was dead."

"And I was cleared."

"Yes, if she'd brought it to our attention before we found Busch, we might have figured you were there and struggled with Payne. Worst case, we might have thought you tumbled to his plan and beat him to the punch."

"Oh."

He held her by the shoulders. "Thing is, Liz, you could blame Miss Hauser for Rose's death. She knew Mrs. Payne was obsessing about you, held you responsible for her son's death, and had a gun. If Miss Hauser had alerted us sooner, maybe all of this could have been avoided."

Liz stared at him, nodding slightly.

The sliding glass door to the house slid open. "Hey, you two, dinner's ready. Miriam's invited us to stay, Jim," Eileen said. She closed the sliding door and disappeared from view.

Shannon glanced at Liz as if to be sure she was okay with the invitation. Liz nodded, and, with Shannon's arm around her, they retreated to the house.

✂❦THIRTY-FIVE❦✂

DINNER CONVERSATION TOUCHED on Gerald's prize roses. Looking at this balding, freckled fire plug of a man, Shannon smiled at the thought of him nurturing the lovely flowers in their garden. Gerald looked more like one of the rough teamsters at Shannon Trucking. However, it was evident from the way the tough little Irishman's features softened when he glanced at her that he adored his regal wife. Perhaps cultivating roses was a work of art he'd created to honor this woman. Miriam touched Gerald's hand and glanced at him often during the conversation.

Both Miriam and Liz talked about Paddy's work, how talented he was, and that they wanted to publish his book. Just as Miriam and Liz rose from the table to bring dessert to the table, the doorbell rang. Miriam and Gerald eyed each other.

"Well, Gerald, I guess the only way to find out who's at our door is to answer it."

They grinned at each other. Gerald nodded and rose to answer the door while Miriam and Liz set the dishes of Peach Melba on the table.

Gerald came back quickly with Paddy and three women Liz recognized from Paddy's family photographs. Liz searched her memory for the sisters' names. They fell into place. The one named Vonnie hung back from the rest. Liz guessed that one was reserving judgment.

"Uh. These folks were concerned about you, Liz, and insisted on seeing you," Gerald said. He looked at Liz as though begging her to say it was okay that he let them in.

Eileen looked at them in surprise. "What are all of you doing here?"

The four glanced at each other as though coming here might have been a mistake.

Paddy spoke for them. "Mom, when you phoned me about what happened and that you were coming here to make sure Liz was okay, I just couldn't wait around. So I rounded up the girls—" He caught his sisters' raised eyebrows. "Sorry, I called my *sisters* and told them what happened. I just couldn't wait to hear from you that she was alright."

Vonnie cleared her throat. "I really didn't think this was such a good idea, but I was outnumbered." She glanced at the table. "It looks like you're in the middle of dinner. Maybe we should leave." She caught her brother's eye. "Paddy, it looks like she's okay."

Her siblings said nothing, but Maura was the one who rolled her eyes this time. Miriam rose and headed toward the kitchen. "There's more than enough room for four more at the table. Sit. Join us for coffee and Peach Melba." It sounded more like an order than an invitation.

Gerald glanced at the group, nodded, and escaped to the kitchen to help Miriam.

They arranged themselves at the table, and Liz noticed that Vonnie sat the furthest from her.

"Uncle Jim, I'm so sorry about Rose," Paddy said. His sisters added their regrets.

Shannon looked down at his plate, nodding. No one spoke for a moment. Finally, Eileen filled the gap. "Well, this wasn't exactly how I planned to introduce you all, but I guess this is as good a time as any." She rose, went to Vonnie, and placed her hands on her shoulders. "This is my oldest, Siobhan, or Vonnie as she prefers to be called."

Vonnie smiled briefly and nodded. "Few people can pronounce, let alone spell, 'Siobhan.'"

"It was my grandmother's name. My mother's mother." Eileen said. "And this is Erin."

"I'm so glad you're okay, and we finally get to meet you." Her eyes were warm.

"And I'm Maura," she said before Eileen could introduce her.

Eileen shrugged. "I think I'll go see if Miriam and Gerald need an extra pair of hands."

"Gosh, you look so much like Dad," Maura said. "Oh, except you're much prettier."

Liz laughed. Had she grown up in this family, she was sure this one would have been her shadow.

"Now, you really look like Dad with that gap between your teeth! Just like Paddy, too."

"Maura," Vonnie said.

"I'm sorry. I guess I'm being rude. It's just that . . . well, I'm so excited to meet you."

"That's fine. Don't worry about it." Liz said. She looked at Vonnie. "I suppose things will be a little awkward for awhile, but I hope not for long."

Vonnie appeared not to have heard this last comment. Shannon raised an eyebrow and stared at her. Just as the silence was becoming awkward, Eileen, Miriam, and Gerald carried in the dessert and coffee service. Eileen introduced her daughters to Miriam and Gerald, and everyone settled into eating the dessert, each savoring it, and all momentarily lost in thought, except for the occasional appraising glance at Liz.

Erin sipped her coffee. "Uncle Jimmy, which funeral home is taking care of Rose?"

"Carter's in the West End. Captain McIlheny said Carmine Luissi—you remember Luissi from the crime scene, Liz?" She nodded. "Carmine is helping Rose's mother with the arrangements. I would guess the viewing begins tomorrow. The service will probably be at St. Philip's, but I don't know when." He smiled sadly as though remembering something funny. "With Luissi organizing it, you can be sure everything will be perfect." He swallowed hard and cleared his throat, his eyes beginning to water.

"We'll be there, Uncle Jimmy," Erin said, beginning to tear up herself.

Liz closed her eyes. She remembered how very hard it was to walk into the funeral home and see her mother in that casket. It had been one of the hardest things she'd done in her life. Shannon had lost his parents in a car accident, his brother-in-law and, worst of all, his wife and child. She didn't think losing people got any easier. And she couldn't help feeling responsible for his latest loss. She hesitated, then reached over and touched his hand. He took her hand and gently squeezed it, smiling at her.

"Well, I think it's time we made our way home. But before we go, let us help you clean up, Miriam," Eileen said.

"Not necessary. Gerald and Liz will lend a hand. They always do."

As they got up from the table, Liz touched Eileen's arm. "Would you all like to see Gerald's rose garden? It's still light out. Believe me, it's quite an experience."

"Of course." Eileen looked at her daughters and they all nodded. Paddy shrugged.

As Gerald led them along the many paths around his roses, explaining the different varieties and pointing out his own hybrids, Liz gradually fell back until she was beside Vonnie. "Would you like to see the gazebo? I used to spend a lot of time there when I lived with the Kernans."

Vonnie glanced at her. She looked like she might say "no."

"Alright."

As they entered the gazebo, Vonnie looked around nodding. "I can see why you spent so much time here."

"Their son Michael told me that Gerald had it built for me because he thought I needed a place just to be alone."

"Wasn't Michael jealous?"

"No. It's not there anymore, but he and Gerald built a tree house way in the back corner of the property a few years before I came to live with them, and their daughter Esther had no interest in having her own spot in the garden."

"Where are their children?"

Liz grinned. "Michael is a rabbi in New York City and Esther is now Sister Mary Ignatius Loyola of the Sisters of Mercy. She teaches math at an all-girls school in Rochester."

Vonnie's mouth dropped open. "You're kidding me!" Liz shook her head. "How? It's a joke, right? You're trying to loosen me up."

"I admit it. I'm trying to loosen you up, but it's no joke. Miriam is Jewish, a concentration camp survivor. She and Gerald met when the Army assigned him to work with displaced people at one of the refugee camps. He worked with her a long time to try to find family or friends, but no one she knew had survived. By the time they figured that out, they were—I don't want to say hopelessly in love—more like hopefully in love, considering what she'd been through."

The sun was slowly making its way to the horizon, and the crickets began their late summer serenade.

"Being named Miriam, I thought she might be Jewish, but Gerald Kernan has got to be Irish—and this being Pittsburgh, Irish Catholic. I thought a non-Catholic had to convert or at least agree to raise any children Catholic."

Liz grinned. "Well, let's just say Gerald has his ways. They did send Michael and Esther to Catholic school and took them to mass. But Friday evenings, the whole family went to Synagogue. They also encouraged discussion at the dinner table and taught their children to think for themselves. I enjoyed those times with the Kernans while I was at Pitt."

"Hm. And to think you might have spent that time with us."

"Is that what's bothering you?"

"No—I don't know." Vonnie looked out at the garden. "Mom told me when I was born, and Dad first held me, he cried. We always thought it was because he was so happy to have me." She glanced back at Liz. "Now, I wonder if having me made him remember you, and that he wasn't crying because he was so happy to have me, but because he'd never seen or held you. And then finding out about his awful childhood and how he rejected you when you found him. I had a hard time putting all that together with the father who made me feel so special."

Liz shrugged and shook her head.

Vonnie chuckled. "This is going to sound childish, but it's important to me. I'm now no longer the oldest—the go to sister. I always felt special being the first. In fact, when I was little, I always thought I was Dad's favorite. Of course, since I now have two of my own, I know we were all special to him."

"Well, you know, you grew up with them. In their eyes you are still the oldest. Nothing can change that bond. Really, you might say that I'm just the incidental daughter—and since he and I only met once, there's no way I can compete with you being special to him."

Vonnie shook her head and looked at Liz like she'd sprouted a third eye. "Incidental daughter? Weird."

Then she studied Liz as though she wanted to be sure this new-found sibling wasn't being condescending. Her face softened into a gentle smile and she nodded. "I guess you're okay. Yeah, you're okay. . . . I'm sorry you missed out on the better part of Dad."

Maura popped into the gazebo. "Here you are. Mom wants to know if we're driving Paddy back to the dorm, or do we want her to take him."

Vonnie stretched as she got up. "I'll go tell her we'll take him back. See you soon, Liz."

Maura looked around the gazebo. "Nice digs."

Liz smiled at this impish sister with a paint smear on her shirt sleeve.

"I'm glad we have a minute alone together. I don't know what Paddy told you about us, but I just wanted to let you know that I'm pretty sure I was Dad's favorite. I'm only telling you this because I think if you had lived with us, hands down, you would have been his favorite."

Her effervescence faded. "I was angry at him for not claiming you. It was hard to accept he'd do something like that. He was such a big man. You know what I mean?"

Liz nodded. "I'm beginning to see that."

"We all looked up to him. It's hard to believe he could be so scared, he'd do that." She broke into a huge smile. "But I'm so glad we found you, and I think it's wonderful you and Uncle Jimmy are seeing each other. He's been so sad and lonely."

"Maura! We're leaving," Vonnie called out.

Maura scampered away and Liz followed.

The last to leave were Eileen and Shannon. "Liz, there's something you need to know about my daughters—and your father. He had a remarkable gift for making each of them feel like she was his favorite. Right, Jimmy?"

"He certainly did."

"And Paddy?" Liz asked.

Eileen chuckled. "Oh, Paddy thinks because he's the only boy and the youngest that he's everyone's favorite. But I've always made it clear to all of them that I have no favorites. Anyway, if they bring it up, don't disabuse them."

"My lips are sealed, but Vonnie let me know she understands they were all special to him."

Eileen registered mild surprise and then satisfaction.

Shannon hugged Liz and kissed the top of her head. "I'll let you know about Rose's viewing and funeral mass."

"Okay."

When she closed the door on them, the feeling of being left in a void was only relieved by the sounds of Gerald and Miriam working in the kitchen.

ͤ**THIRTY–SIX**ͤ

"YOU DON'T DRIVE?" Paddy asked Liz while Eileen looked for a parking space near the Santello home.

"No, I do, but I've found it much easier to get around town by cab. It gives me a chance to relax instead of second-guessing clueless drivers." She caught Eileen's glance in the rearview mirror. "I'm sorry. I should have offered to drive instead of expecting you to pick me up."

"Not a problem," Eileen said and smiled.

Paddy glanced back with a smile. "I just wanted to know if you knew how."

Shannon, sitting next to her in the back, patted her hand.

A slender, dark-haired boy stepped into the street from the Santello driveway and signaled them to turn in. The large manicured lawn had been turned into a parking lot complete with sprayed lines.

"I see Luissi has everything under control," Shannon said with raised eyebrows.

"Won't the lawn be ruined?" asked Liz.

"Knowing Luissi, the landscaper will be here early tomorrow morning. He'll find some way for the department to pick up the tab, too."

At first glance, the house resembled an Italian villa. However, Liz realized, though suitable for a large family, it was constructed on a smaller scale of well-set faded red brick and, instead of a tiled roof, had asphalt shingles similar to its neighbors. She knew there would be a large vegetable garden in the backyard and maybe some grape arbors for home-brewed grappa.

As they exited the car, conversations in Italian reached them through the open windows. The lilting sounds reminded Liz of her childhood when so many immigrants in the small communities surrounding Pittsburgh spoke more often in their native tongue than in English. She could hear the shouts and laughter of smaller children who had been banished to the backyard. When they entered the home, Liz found many of the people who were at the funeral, some leaving while others like themselves were arriving. Among the later arrivals, she spotted her sisters and a few other people who looked like they might be from the Shannon clan.

Family and neighbors had overwhelmed the dining room table with offerings of antipasti, gnocchi, lasagna, ravioli, cannelloni, calamari, breads, cheeses, salami, sardines, olives, peppers and pickles. A long buffet offered strong coffee, grappa, soft drinks, fruit, anise cookies, biscotti, angel wings, hazelnut chocolates and some desserts Liz did not recognize. She'd been too nervous to eat this morning, but now the enticing scents roused her hunger to the point where she almost headed for the food before again paying her respects to Rose's mother and grandmother.

She caught Shannon looking at her with a knowing smile. "Hungry?"

She blushed. "It was so kind of Rose's grandmother to insist I come to the house after the funeral. What is her name again?"

"Mrs. Florentino."

She saw Eileen and Paddy were already talking with Mrs. Santello and Rose's grandmother, who were surrounded by a gaggle of people, probably relatives. Luissi seemed to appear and disappear in different parts of the two rooms. He surveyed the action and occasionally gestured to younger family members to correct whatever he found wanting. Shannon told her that Luissi and Rose were cousins, and he had helped Rose get on the force. Liz wondered if Luissi, too, felt some responsibility for Rose's death.

Men and women in uniform—as was Shannon—milled among other guests and swarmed the spotless living room which was furnished with dark Mediterranean furniture. Beneath the scents from the dining room wafted the faint odor of furniture polish. They wove through the crowd, and his fellow policemen stopped Shannon to ask how he was doing and wish him a speedy return to the job. Shannon thanked them and nodded. Apparently, it wasn't common knowledge that Shannon was leaving the force—or was he? Perhaps Rose's death, instead of solidifying his resolve to leave, was causing him to reconsider his decision.

Mrs. Santello and her mother glanced up when Liz and Shannon approached. Grief had grayed them and sketched deeper lines into their faces since the morning funeral mass and burial. Mrs. Santello, unlike Mrs. Florentino, was tall and slender with streaks of gray in her short, thick, dark hair. Her eyes, the color of sherry, seemed to be looking at something far away, but livened when she saw Shannon.

Rose had inherited her short, stocky build from her grandmother. The older lady wore her snow-white hair in a bun at the back of her neck and gazed at them with intense dark eyes. Both women wore black, loose-fitting dresses and clutched large snowy handkerchiefs in their hands.

Mrs. Florentino's eyes lightened when she saw Liz. "Umma so glad you comma to our house. Our Rosa, she woulda be so glad, too." She glanced at her daughter. "*Sì*, Antonia?"

Mrs. Santello nodded.

"People say Rosa, she die too soon. I say no, we alla have our time, whatta you call it? Uh . . . *destino*."

"She means 'destiny,'" said Mrs. Santello.

"*Il mio destino* to live lotta years. Umma eighty-seven next month." She shook her head. "*Stupido* peasant like me living long time. Rosa, so smart, so *coraggio*, she die so young. Not always make the sense. *Destino*."

She took Liz's hand into her dry, gnarled ones. "Our Rosa live to save people like you." The old woman nodded. "She like you so much. She tell us how you worka so hard, how you so smart, and how you have so much bad things in you life."

Mrs. Florentino sat up straighter. "You comma from people like us. You do good because you worka and have the heart—not sit around like lazy people, like stuck-up money people. Umma so happy she die fora protect you. Notta some—whatta you call it? Uh . . . *si*, somma junkie."

She looked off at the rest of the room for a moment and then back at Liz. "You show alla them people, peasants have somma smarts and not afraid to work." She looked long at Liz, then nodded. "*Si*, you looka like Mona."

"Mamma." Mrs. Santello said.

Mrs. Florentino shook her head. "Our Rosa, not like other girls, but she was good girl. Umma gonna miss her. But you . . ." she patted Liz's hand, "you make me feel better. You good girl, too." Tears sprang to her eyes, and Rose's mother sobbed as well.

Tears threatened to spill from Liz's eyes. "I feel so bad." She looked at Mrs. Santello. "I feel like it's my fault, and I wish I could go back and make it different."

"No! Itta not you fault! No, no! Itta *destino*!" Mrs. Florentino said.

"She's right. It's not your fault that crazy woman killed her, any more than it's Carmine's fault because he helped her become a police officer," Mrs. Santello said, wiping her eyes. "Our Rose wasn't afraid to be true to who she was, even though she knew many people would hate her for it."

Liz looked puzzled.

"It was harder for her to become a detective than it was for the men, especially since she wasn't like other women. And she knew being a police officer was dangerous work. She'd been shot before and had a long, hard recovery. But she went back anyway."

Mrs. Santello got that distant look in her eyes again. "When she was little, she always took up for the kids who got picked on. She believed she was born to protect those who can't defend themselves." She looked at Shannon. "And she got a lot out of putting away the bad guys. Right, Jimmy?"

He nodded. Liz could see he was choked up.

"Jeemmy," Mrs. Florentino began, "Rosa say you wanna quit. No. You no quit. You like Rosa, a *soldato*. You no quit, Jeemmy."

"Mamma, it's none of your business," Mrs. Santello said.

"It's okay," Shannon said.

Mrs. Santello stood up and hugged Shannon. "You're a good man, Jimmy. Rose trusted you. She always thought of you like the kid brother she never had."

Shannon smiled and nodded. "Yeah, sometimes I felt like her kid brother."

"How are you doing, Jimmy?"

"Better each day."

She took both their hands and squeezed them. "Please, stay and have some food."

"*Si, mangia, mangia,*" Mrs. Florentino said.

Liz thanked them both, and Shannon bent down to kiss Mrs. Florentino's cheek. "*Grazie,*" he whispered.

She nodded and grabbed his hand. "You will be good *soldato*. Rosa, she watcha over you now."

Making their way to the dining room, they were waylaid by a bony, middle-aged little woman with short, fading red hair. "I'm so sorry about Rose, Jimmy. How you doing?"

"Fine, Katelyn." She smiled and looked expectantly at Liz. "Oh, this is Liz Michaels, the new cousin in the family. Liz, Katelyn O'Brien."

"Yes, I thought it might be you. You look so much like Ivy." She stepped back and looked Liz up and down. "But you don't look like someone who runs a magazine stand."

Vonnie, who had been right behind Katelyn, interrupted. "Katelyn, Liz runs a publishing company. In fact, she's one of the owners."

"Oh, why was I told she sold magazines?"

"The old unreliable telephone tree, Katelyn."

"Un-huh." She brightened and took Liz's hand. "Well, so glad to meet you. I'm sure we'll be seeing each other again soon."

As Katelyn disappeared into the crowd, Shannon said, "Thanks, Vonnie."

"Telephone tree?" Liz said.

"We have this set up in the family whenever anything important needs to be communicated to everyone. Mom starts it by calling her sisters, and they pass the news on to the people on their lists, and those people pass it on down the line. I won't tell you what Katelyn was told when you ended up in the hospital, Uncle Jimmy," she said, rolling her eyes.

"Well, I need to get going. Mom's planning another girls-only brunch for us, so see you then."

She reached into her purse. "Here's my card with my home number. I added Erin's and Maura's numbers on the back. Mom gave us yours. Call us any time." She hugged Shannon, hesitated, and then hugged Liz before she swept off into the crowd to gather her two sisters.

"Looks like Vonnie's getting used to the idea of having an older sister," Shannon said. "Vonnie can be intimidating, but once she takes you on, you've got a friend for life. Let's get something to eat before Eileen rounds us up."

"I second that."

They found a secluded spot in the backyard and ate. Shannon broke the silence after he emptied his plate. "Are you up for seconds?"

"No, but you go right ahead."

"I think I'll take it easy on the food since I haven't had much exercise."

"You still look pretty fit," Liz said. She looked down at her empty plate and then back up at Shannon. "Uh, Jim?"

"Yes?"

"What did Mrs. Santello mean when she said Rose was true to herself even if it meant some people wouldn't like it?"

Shannon drained his cup, put it down, and looked at her as though he couldn't believe she had missed something important. "You didn't pick up on it?"

"Pick up on what?"

"Rose was a lesbian."

Liz's eyes widened. "Now, what was it about her that was supposed to broadcast her sexual preference? She just seemed like a tough police officer who didn't like me very much early on."

"Yeah, I guess to most people that's how she came across. I will tell you, though, I think she was so antagonistic towards you because she was attracted to you. You're slender and blond like Mona. After Mona died, she used to always get into that love-hate mode whenever she met an attractive woman who looked like Mona."

Liz looked off to the garden at the back of the property. "Mona. She called me that right before she died. Who was Mona?"

"I guess you'd say they were soul mates. They lived together for a number of years, never looked at anyone else. A few years ago—this was before I lost Angie—Mona developed uterine cancer. Rose nursed her through it until Mona died. She'd never found anyone since." He grinned. "She was kidding, but she said if I struck out with you, she'd try her luck."

"I'm afraid I would have disappointed her."

"Aw, she was just egging me on. She knew you were straight."

Liz recalled how the peppery little woman gave her such a hard time and smiled.

Shannon cleared his throat. "You know, we haven't had that dinner date I promised you."

"This doesn't count?"

"No-o-o. How about tomorrow?"

"Let's make it the day after. I have some catching up to do at the office. And I'll drive. Is six good for you?"

"No, let's make it five. I think we have a lot to talk about."

She caught the meaning in his eyes and nodded.

⚡THIRTY-SEVEN⚡

ABE PERKINS INCHED into the conference room, which served as Liz's temporary office. Mandy followed, hidden behind a substantial floral arrangement cascading from a large crystal vase. She placed the flowers in the middle of the table and grinned at Liz before leaving.

"Hello, Abe."

Abe nodded. "Liz, how are you?" He retrieved the card from the bouquet, pulled out one of the chairs from the table, and slid it before Liz's desk. He hesitated, then proffered the card before sitting in the chair.

Liz read it. "In appreciation for all you've done to make this sale happen." Unsmiling, she placed the card on her desk. "Are you sure you don't need more time, Abe? Maybe wait until *all* the gossip has died down?"

Abe, who could be mistaken for an Ivy League college dean, lowered his hazel eyes and pinked. He then glanced up. "I am so sorry, Liz. I couldn't believe all the things my wife heard, but she heard it from respectable people."

"Respectable people like Eunice Payne?"

He swallowed and looked away.

"How long have you known me, Abe?"

He returned his gaze to her. "Since you worked for the Kernans at their print shop."

She stared at this well-preserved, white-haired man. "And through all these years, did you ever consider me less than respectable?"

"Liz, you know I've held you in the highest regard. You are a leader in this industry. You've taken risks on writers that few of us considered marketable and turned their work into bestsellers." He snorted. "What still rankles me is you've published the best history of Pennsylvania to date."

"Yes, your editors missed the boat on that one."

He shook his head. "Oh, and I've never let them forget it. You do incredible things. You've made niche markets like New Age books profitable. And you've managed to create all this success while keeping everyone involved happy. You're a model of the fair business person who subscribes to the highest professional standards. That's always been my belief."

"Pretty words, Abe."

"All true."

"Yet you were willing to believe that my personal life wasn't up to the same high standards."

He looked down at manicured nails. "I don't know what to say."

"Abe, I was prepared to cut all ties with Kernan, Feinstein and Company—to end my career—so that the sale could go through without a hitch—all because of vicious rumors, which you thought could be true."

He raised his eyes to her. "I feel horrible about all this. I'm sorry I doubted you. Please accept my apology."

She smirked at the floral arrangement. "Pretty posies. Couldn't you find a bigger bouquet?"

Abe barely grinned. "My wife ordered them, but I thought I should bring the flowers to you in person and apologize."

She leaned back in her chair. "Well, I'll give you that. However, if we're to work together over the next couple of years, I need to feel I have your full confidence."

"Understood." He rose and replaced the chair at the table. "So you'll be there with Gerald tomorrow to sign the contract?"

"Of course. Company bylaws require two of the three principals who are not related or married to each other to sign any contract involving sizeable amounts of money."

He chuckled and took her hand. "I hope, in time, you won't think so badly of me."

"Everyone deserves a second chance—certainly old friends deserve at least that."

He squeezed her hand, nodded, and left.

❧

Miriam entered the conference room, newspaper in hand, and frowned at the over-the-top flowers. She read the card and chuckled. "I see Abe has made his mea culpa. I suppose he couldn't write, 'forgive me for thinking you might be a murderer.'"

Liz smiled. "We both knew the flowers weren't about my work on the sale. We made peace."

Miriam pulled out a chair and sat. "Have you seen this morning's *Post Gazette*?"

"No."

Miriam handed her the paper and pointed to the article on the front page headlined, "Socialite from Respected Ohio Family Killed While Attempting Assault."

Liz read the article, and by the time she reached the end of it, she was beaming. It was a detailed account of Eunice's attack on her resulting in Rose's death, the discovery that Addy had broken into her home using a lock pick, and that documents had surfaced suggesting he intended to kill her so he could collect on a life insurance policy. The article finished on an inside page. Next to it, another article presenting Liz's career accomplishments as well as a list of charities she sponsored appeared along with a picture of her working at a charitable event. Also on the same page, another article memorialized Rose Santello's life.

"Hm. Don't you think the article on me is a little overkill? Where did they get all the details—and the picture?"

Miriam raised her eyebrows and gave a little shrug of her shoulders. "Darnley himself called for the information. I suppose it's the editor's way of letting us know he always believed in your innocence. Didn't he want to date you once?"

"Yes, but I couldn't date a man whose divorce wasn't final. As it is, they're back together again—and expecting." Liz's eyes twinkled. "I wonder what the *Tattler* story will be."

"Who cares?"

"You're right. Miriam." Liz reached for her purse. "Let's go to Vinaigrette for a very long lunch."

"Oh, yes. Perhaps some of Eunice Payne's friends will be there, dining on crow cordon bleu."

"Do you think we're being insensitive?"

Miriam stood a little taller. "Eating lunch at our favorite restaurant is our right. Nothing insensitive about that."

❦❦THIRTY–EIGHT❦❦

LIZ BRAKED HER black '79 Camry a moment to stare at the Tudor-style home where her father and Eileen had raised their family. Other than the trees and shrubs having matured, it hadn't changed from her first sight of it when she was nineteen-year-old Liz Migielski, the lonely girl who couldn't bring herself to approach the oak front door.

She pulled into the wide driveway, stopping short of the flagstone sidewalk leading to the house. She glanced into the rearview mirror to check her makeup and hair and noticed her mother and grandmother were gone, although the scent of vanilla lingered. They'd trailed her everywhere the past two days. And they'd been in her dreams, but she only remembered glimpsing them and awakening feeling reassured. Odd. She couldn't recall their being around her this much in the past.

Before she could ring the bell, Shannon whipped open the door, a ruffled, blue gingham apron grasped in his other hand. She took in the tall man in navy suit pants, crisp white shirt, and blue paisley tie. A lock of his dark hair quivered over his forehead, and his face was flushed. He looked her up and down, but stopped at whistling. She was glad she'd worn the blue, raw silk dress that hugged her slender frame and matched the color of her eyes.

"You look great," he said, "but you always do."

Liz drew back and squinted at him.

"Well, you have every time I've seen you."

"Thank you. Are you ready to go?"

"Sort of. Come in." He glanced at her car as he closed the door. "You know, I figured you for a BMW or a Mercedes."

"My Bentley's in the shop."

He raised his eyebrows at her.

"Okay, I'm pulling your leg. My identity isn't wrapped up in the kind of car I drive. To me, a car is just something to get me where I want to go." Her eyes widened as she sniffed the air. "What is that wonderful smell? Some kind of beef dish, isn't it?"

He grinned down at her. "That's our dinner."

"Oh, you cooked?"

"I could lie and say I did, but then you'd expect me to whip up great food from here on out. No, Eileen made our mom's traditional Irish stew and soda bread. But I did put together the salad and dressing. I couldn't think of a better place than Eileen's for really good Irish food. Besides, it's quieter here."

"So, where is Eileen?"

"She and Vonnie went out to dinner and are going to see *On Golden Pond*."

"Didn't that film open last year?"

"There's a theater in Squirrel Hill that shows older releases. Last week, it was *Ordinary People*." Shannon took her purse, laid it on a table in the foyer, and then guided her to the dining room. "Would you like some wine?"

"That would be nice."

Liz sat in the chair he pulled out for her.

"You know, I used to do this for my sisters. But every now and again, I'd pull the chair out from under them."

She laughed. "You were something else, weren't you?"

"Yeah, but so were they. I stopped doing it after I woke up with my fingernails and toenails painted neon pink."

After Shannon went to the kitchen for the wine, Liz studied the room. The walls looked like they had been freshly painted a pale cream. Dark cherry hardwood floors gleamed, and beneath the table lay an Aubusson rug. The long table, chairs, server, and massive china cabinet were in a dark traditional style that reminded her of the stuff of Irish castles; and their patina revealed that someone had lovingly maintained them. Irish linen and Waterford crystal adorned the table. Liz turned over a plate, validating what she suspected. The china was Belleek. A simple arrangement of pink, pale peach, and cream roses in a low crystal bowl graced the center of the table guarded by two ornate silver candlesticks.

So this was where her father and his family shared their meals, their laughter. What a contrast to the meals of her own childhood. Liz was surprised to realize she felt no bitterness or regret. Maybe the hard times made her the capable, successful person she was today.

Shannon returned, lit the candles, and poured the wine. He held his glass out to her in a toast, his eyes brightened by the candlelight. "To new beginnings."

Liz smiled and clinked glasses with him. "To new beginnings." She sipped the velvety wine and put her glass down.

"Hungry?"

Liz stared at the centerpiece. "The roses are beginning to look absolutely delicious."

"Be back in a jiffy."

"Need any help?"

"No. Just relax." Then he grinned. "But when I get back, I'll be counting the roses."

Liz watched him disappear into the kitchen. He not only had a sense of humor but was a fine looking man from the back as well as the front.

Following a dinner that lived up to its promise, they took their coffee into the living room. Liz surveyed the room and imagined her father in the corner recliner, perhaps watching Paddy crawling to him. She glimpsed the pictures on the mantle and got up to take a closer look.

There was the old, faded photograph of his unsmiling mother, bearing features that were like her own. In a family photograph that included her father, she saw a man who did look happy, not the stern stranger she had encountered when she was nineteen. She would like to have known that man. The photo of Jim and Angie evoked a pang of envy but also saddened her. They both looked so happy. She told herself it was silly to be jealous of a dead woman. The man had a big heart; he could love again, but he would never forget his dead wife. Liz wouldn't have him any other way.

"It must feel strange to you being here. I hope it doesn't make you uncomfortable."

She returned to the floral-patterned sofa. "No. Maybe a little sad. I would have liked to get to know him, to see him here with the others. My only contact with him was that one meeting, and I don't guess either of us handled it well. Maybe I should have accepted his job offer at the insurance company. In time, he might have felt more confident about introducing me to the family."

"It's hard to say. He'd lost so much, and fear is a tough emotion to conquer. Ei always says fear is the root of all evil."

"That makes a lot of sense. If Addy hadn't been so afraid he'd never again be successful, would he have planned to kill me?"

"I'm not so sure it was fear motivating him so much as narcissism. Remember what I told you about how he charmed and manipulated the people at that bar to get what he wanted? Wouldn't surprise me if he might have been a psychopath, not just narcissistic." Shannon paused. "But, then again, I guess he did feel the image he had of himself was threatened."

"In the beginning, Addy was so attentive. He did all the right things to make me feel like I was the center of his universe." Liz sighed. "But that didn't last long. It was such a letdown to discover that I'd married a man who thought only of himself."

Shannon stared into his coffee, cleared his throat, and then gazed at her. "Anyone can tell you that, with me, what you see is what you get."

She returned his gaze and nodded. "I can believe that. And the same with me. I don't have the time or the energy for games."

"So, us? It's a go?"

"Don't you think we've already made that decision?"

He nodded. "I wasn't sure if *you* knew that. However, there's something that might make a difference to you?"

"Yes?"

"I've decided to stay with the force."

"Why does that not surprise me?"

"You and Santello seem to know me better than I know myself. I know I'm good at what I do, and I'm needed. I have a passion for the work—not exactly like Santello—but I know I make a difference. Santello told me I had a calling, and God would snatch me back if I left the force. She had that calling, and dying for the cause made me see how it made what she did with her life that much more meaningful. Staying the course honors her memory."

He stared at the cup in his hands. "Eileen and I talked. She says I just have to get more balance in my life. Actually, she told me I need to get a life." He smirked. "Besides, I looked around and realized that more homicide detectives ended up retiring than dying in the line of duty."

"We all make the choices we need to for a fulfilling life. You'll never hear me badger you about quitting the force."

"Even though there's always the possibility that the worst could happen?"

"Maybe the odds are greater for people in your line of work, but the worst could happen to any of us at any time. I think the trick is living life fully aware, one day at a time, and never taking all the loving people in your life for granted."

He nodded and sighed.

"Of course, my work is my passion, too. It's a part of me and not something I could ever give up. The same goes for my name. I may not care about the kind of car I drive, but the name I chose is very important to me."

"And you shouldn't have to give any of it up. How do you feel about children?"

She grinned. "Hey, Detective. This is only our first date."

He blushed and fiddled with his cup. "I feel like we've known each other a long time."

She rested her hand on his. "I know what you mean. . . . I've always wanted children. After what happened with Addy, though, I thought I'd pretty much missed out on the chance of being a mother."

He took her coffee and set it with his own on the cocktail table. Then he placed her hand in both of his. "Let's agree that no matter how this turns out, we'll have no regrets—and that you'll always be a part of this family."

Liz smiled and nodded. Shannon pulled her into his arms. He caressed her soft cheek, looked long into the eyes that had possessed him the first time he saw her, and kissed her. It was a very long kiss, a pledge of things to come. The scent of vanilla enveloped them, and Liz knew she had finally come home.

ᎦᏍ ACKNOWLEDGMENTS ᏍᎦ

It takes a village to raise a child—and to produce a book. I am ever so grateful to my writing community, including my critique group: Bethany Mackin Baxter, author of *Two Sons*; Reverie Escobedo, an extraordinary teacher and writer; and John Meeks, author of *Bogey's Final Gift* and *Bogey's Mortal Lock*. You patiently and kindly gave me insightful advice and encouraged me. I've learned so much from you. I also very much appreciate the editorial assistance of Priscilla Digue and Kendra Pritsi.

I owe a special thank you to Sunny Fader, an established script writer, documentary film maker, and author of *Land Here, You Bet!* and *The Cat Who Loved Dogs*, for her encouragement and her advice on PR copy. She and Ceceann Harway, also a script writer and film maker, have long been my mentors.

The feedback of my beta readers helped me see what would work and not work for readers of my novel. They are Kelly Brady, Maxine Davenport, Carol Fowler, Pam Hutchison, Wanda Petrich, Judi Rollins, Karen Russell, and Jan Weatherford.

A writer relies on many kinds of resources. I have found the following invaluable: *Self-Editing for Fiction Writers: How to Edit Yourself into Print*, Second Edition, by Renni Browne and Dave King; *Revising Fiction: Making Sense of the Madness* by Kirt Hickman; *The Chicago Manual of Style*, 15th Edition; *The Fine Print of Self-Publishing*, Fourth Edition by Mark Levine; Joel Friedlander's website (thebookdesigner.com); articles from *Poets and Writers*, *The Writer*, and *Writer's Digest*; The New Mexico Book Association; The New Mexico Book Co-op; Southwest Writers; and the folks at CreateSpace who helped me physically produce and distribute the book you now hold in your hands. Any fault you find with this novel is entirely my responsibility.

ᚻᚱ**POSTSCRIPT**ᚱᚻ

I have exercised fictional license throughout this book and ask that any readers who know better, or might take offense, accept my apologies.

The Terrace Room in the William Penn Hotel is real, and to this day, continues to serve very fine food. Kernan's Print Shop in Carnegie exists only in the landscape of my imagination as does The Lafayette atop Mt. Washington; Busch's Tavern in Southside; Kernan, Feinstein and Company; William Penn Press; the theater in Squirrel Hill that shows older films; Angelino's; and Vinaigrette—although there is a Vinaigrette in Santa Fe. Shannon Trucking companies exist in other parts of the country, but I have been unable to find evidence of such a company in Pittsburgh in 1982. The Steinmetz bakery, of which I have fond memories, closed in the late eighties. Also, that striking PPG glass cathedral building didn't exist until 1984. However, it's such a dramatic, well-recognized Pittsburgh landmark these days, I couldn't resist including it.

Although it's been popularly held that the Black Irish descend from Spaniards who washed ashore during the Spanish Armada, genetic research discounts that theory. If you are interested, you may explore the many theories about the origins of the Black Irish online.

All of the characters inhabit only my imagination and in no way represent any person, living or dead. However, the first governor of Ohio really was Edward Tiffin, an upstanding and talented man of his time. I could find no mention of the governor's progeny; but I hope that any genuine descendants will pardon me for giving them such repugnant relatives.

Thank You

Thank you for allowing me to share Liz's story with you. If you enjoyed this story, please feel free to leave a brief review and rating at Amazon.com. Amazon only requires a minimum of twenty words. Reviews and ratings help other readers make choices, and positive reviews go a long way to promote the work of indie authors. The same would apply if you bought the book from another online retailer. Of course, word-of-mouth is the best advertising, so do recommend the book to friends you think would enjoy Liz's story.

In the Works

Café Destiny The producers of this webisode series, which I wrote, tell me it should be airing online sometime in the spring of 2013. The website is www.cafe-destiny.com.

Catching Air is the tentative title of my next book and will probably be classified as young adult science fiction, although the story should appeal to adults as well, and the science in the story is not science fiction so much as repressed science. Here is a brief description:

Seventeen-year-old Chet Hain has never escaped feeling guilty for the deaths of his older brother and father when he was ten. The car accident that took his brother's life—and later resulted in his father's death—happened when the family was driving Chet to a skateboard competition. Now, seven years later, Chet notices strangers watching the home he and his mother share. His mother discounts his concerns. However, he will soon learn about his father's work on a readily available source of energy that could have changed the world and the dark conspiracy that seeks to suppress any discoveries that would threaten the power of those who profit from current sources of energy. He uncovers the mystery of the watchers, overcomes his guilt to again compete in skateboard contests, and faces challenges that go far beyond his life as a skater.

To learn more
about what's coming next
or to contact me,
visit my author website:

www.valeriestasik.com

I would enjoy hearing from you.

Val Stasik
January 2013

16866469R00149

Made in the USA
Charleston, SC
14 January 2013